Jeremy Strong

Trouble with Animals

PUFFIN BOOKS

PUFFIN BOOKS

Published by the Penguin Group
Penguin Books Ltd, 80 Strand, London WC2R 0RL, England
Penguin Putnam Inc., 375 Hudson Street, New York, New York 10014, USA
Penguin Books Australia Ltd, 250 Camberwell Road, Camberwell, Victoria 3124, Australia
Penguin Books Canada Ltd, 10 Alcorn Avenue, Toronto, Ontario, Canada M4V 3B2
Penguin Books India (P) Ltd, 11 Community Centre, Panchsheel Park, New Delhi – 110 017, India
Penguin Books (NZ) Ltd, Cnr Rosedale and Airborne Roads, Albany, Auckland, New Zealand
Penguin Books (South Africa) (Pty) Ltd, 24 Sturdee Avenue, Rosebank 2196, South Africa

Penguin Books Ltd, Registered Offices: 80 Strand, London WC2R 0RL, England

www.penguin.com

Trouble with Animals first published by A & C Black (Publishers) Ltd 1980
Text copyright © Jeremy Strong, 1980
Fox on the Roof first published by A & C Black (Publishers) Ltd 1984
Text copyright © Jeremy Strong, 1984
Dogs Are Different first published by A & C Black (Publishers) Ltd 1987
Text copyright © Jeremy Strong, 1987

This collection published as *Trouble with Animals* in Puffin 2001

16

Text copyright © Jeremy Strong, 1980, 1984, 1987, 2001
Illustrations copyright © Nick Sharratt, 2001
All rights reserved

The moral right of the author and illustrator has been asserted

Set in 13½/17 pt PostScript Monotype Baskerville
Typeset by Rowland Phototypesetting Ltd, Bury St Edmunds, Suffolk

Printed in England by Clays Ltd, St Ives plc

British Library Cataloguing in Publication Data
A CIP catalogue record for this book is available from the British Library

ISBN-13: 978-0-14-131005-3

www.greenpenguin.co.uk

Mixed Sources
Product group from well-managed
forests and other controlled sources
www.fsc.org Cert no. SA-COC 1592
©1996 Forest Stewardship Council

Penguin Books is committed to a sustainable future
for our business, our readers and our planet.
The book in your hands is made from paper
certified by the Forest Stewardship Council.

Contents

Trouble with Animals

1 The Rabbit

Tom stood in the kitchen. He had a long piece of string in one hand. In the other he held a large, empty biscuit tin. He watched Mum clearing the table after breakfast.

'How big do you think rabbits are?' he asked at last.

'Some of them grow quite big,' answered Mum.

'Would a rabbit fit in a biscuit tin?'

'Maybe,' Mum replied, without looking at the tin that Tom held up. Mum didn't seem to be very interested. He went outside, trailing the string behind him.

Ever since he was eight, Tom had wanted an animal of his own. Now he was eight

years and two days old. He still did not have
one. He had hoped that Mum and Dad
would give him a horse for his birthday.
They had given him a watch instead. It was a
fantastic watch and Tom was very proud of
it. It was a digital watch with numbers that
shone in the dark. A horse would have been
even more exciting though.

Tom began to think that, if he wanted a
pet, he would have to get one for himself.
There were no ponies on the farm nearby,
but there were plenty of rabbits. Tom
thought that with a tin, a stick, a carrot and
some string he could catch a rabbit easily.

His older sister Jane saw him standing in
the garden with his rabbit-catching
equipment.

'What are you doing?' she asked. 'What do
you want all that for?'

'I'm going to catch a rabbit,' said Tom.

'What do you want a rabbit for?' asked
Jane, wrinkling her nose. 'You can't cook it.
They don't taste nice. I had rabbit pie at
Nicola's for tea last week and it was urrgh!'

'I bet you didn't and I don't want to eat it.
I want to look after it. It's going to be my pet.'

'But they don't do anything,' teased Jane. 'They just scratch themselves and leave dirty messes all over the place. What's the tin for anyway?'

'Well, the rabbit eats the carrot. The carrot is tied to a stick that holds the tin up. When the rabbit eats the carrot he pulls the stick and it slips and the tin falls down bang!' Tom scowled at Jane and added quickly, 'Don't say it doesn't work because it does, so there!'

'Suppose the rabbit isn't under the tin when it falls down bang?' Jane demanded. Tom frowned. He knew his eleven-year-old sister would have some smart answer. He went red.

'The carrot is *under* the tin so the rabbit has *got* to go under to get it,' explained Tom.

Jane rolled her eyes. 'Suppose it's a big rabbit that won't fit? Or a rabbit with extra-long legs that can pull the carrot out?' She bent down and grinned right in Tom's face. 'Or even suppose it's a very clever rabbit that nibbles through the string before it eats the carrot?'

'Rabbits are not that clever,' said Tom staunchly.

'How do you know?'

'Because if they were, they would be able to do lots of other clever things like ride bicycles and play football.'

'You're stupid,' said Jane.

'So are you!'

'Not as stupid as you are,' said Jane with her nose in the air.

'When you see my rabbit you'll be jealous – and stupid!' added Tom as he set off for the fields.

'When I see your rabbit I'll eat it!' Jane shouted after him. 'Stupid yourself!'

Up on the green and brown hillside, Tom hunted amongst the waving grass for burrows. It was most odd. He had often seen burrows and never taken any notice of them. Now that he wanted to find one, they all seemed to have vanished.

Eventually he found two holes. They were close together and sloped down into the bank. Tom knew they were rabbit holes by the messy pile of black pellets outside. He lay on his stomach and peered down each hole in turn. He couldn't see anything. He carefully set up his rabbit trap near the droppings. It was difficult to get the string the right length. Tom tested the trap a couple of times. At last it was ready.

Tom crept away and hid in the long, warm grass. He decided to wait five minutes. A rabbit was bound to come along. He kept looking at his new watch. The minutes seemed to pass very slowly. Tom shook his watch to make sure it had not stopped, but the numbers still flashed at him. Not a single rabbit came.

Tom waited another five minutes and still he did not see one pair of long ears. A sparrow flew down and with a flick of quick wings landed beside the old tin. It bobbed its head and peered around with beady eyes.

Tom wasn't worried about it going near his rabbit trap. Sparrows ate bread, not carrots. Everybody knew that. The sparrow suddenly took a powerful swipe at the carrot with his beak. Tom jumped up. This sparrow did not seem to know that he should leave carrots alone. The sparrow took another great beakful and Tom saw the tin wobble.

'Shoo!' he shouted and clapped his hands. The sparrow took fright and flew off. Tom wondered if a rabbit would mind nibbling a carrot that had been attacked by a sparrow. He looked at his watch. It was almost lunchtime. Five more minutes went. There was still no sign. Tom left the trap and ran home to lunch.

Tom was pleased when lunch was over and he could go back to his rabbit trap. He hurried up the hill. As soon as he reached the burrow he jumped with joy. The tin was down. As he approached it moved. The rusty, red tin shifted around like a small, blind robot. Tom was delighted.

He was about to lift the tin when he suddenly had a terrifying thought. Suppose it was not a rabbit that was making the tin move? Suppose it was a weasel with very sharp teeth? Or an escaped python? Or a deadly poisonous spider?

Tom took a step back and watched the battered tin as it wandered to and fro. Then he thought, it couldn't be a spider. A spider couldn't move a tin that large . . . unless it was a gigantic spider! A python wouldn't fit, so perhaps it was a weasel with sharp teeth?

What was Tom to do? He knew that he would have to lift the tin to catch the animal, but he didn't know what was going to dash out. He sat for a moment, thinking and frowning heavily. He decided that weasels didn't like carrots so it couldn't be that. Then he got a small stick and poked it under one corner. He lifted the tin just a bit. A small nose appeared, and then a tiny pair of eyes. Tom could not see any sharp teeth so he flicked the tin away and jumped back very quickly.

There was a small hedgehog. It looked worried and blinked at Tom. Then it walked straight into one of the rabbit holes and disappeared. Tom picked up the tin and the

string and went sadly home. He left the
carrot for the sparrows.

Mum watched Tom come down the
garden. She saw him throw the tin on to the
rubbish tip.

'Cheer up,' she said. 'You haven't got a
hutch for a rabbit anyway, so you had
nowhere to keep it.'

Tom looked at Mum in surprise. Hutch!
He wasn't going to keep it in a hutch! He
was going to let it wander happily all over
Dad's lettuce patch.

2 A Dog or Two

Tom wandered into Jane's room. She was lying on the floor colouring a large picture. He fiddled with one of her crayons.

'What do you want?' asked Jane. Tom frowned.

'Well, what do you think is the best animal in the world?'

'Can I have my crayon back?' Tom handed it to her. Jane carried on colouring. She was thinking. She knew why Tom was asking. He was still going on about pets and all that rubbish. She smiled and said idly, 'The blue whale. I think they are by far the nicest animals in the whole world.'

Tom sighed. It was not the answer he

wanted to hear. 'Well, what do you think is the second nicest animal in the world then?'

'Another blue whale?' suggested Jane.

'No!' said Tom crossly. 'It's got to be smaller.'

'All right, a slightly smaller blue whale!' teased Jane.

'You're not playing properly,' cried Tom. 'You know what I mean. I mean as a pet.'

'Oh!' said Jane in a loud voice, as if she had never understood. 'You mean a pet.' There was silence for a few moments as she carried on colouring and thought of another animal. 'Boa constrictors,' she said at last. Tom frowned.

'What are boa conductors?'

'Constrictors,' corrected Jane. 'They're big snakes. They grow ever so long and they eat whole goats and pigs in one enormous swallow and they kill their victim by squeezing and squeezing and squeezing it until its heart bursts.'

By the time Jane had finished Tom was by the door. 'I think you're horrible,' he said. 'You're just saying all that on purpose. You know you like dogs.' And with that he hurried downstairs. Jane turned back to her picture. Dogs! Was that what he was after today?

Tom had decided that since rabbits were so difficult to catch he would get himself a dog instead. There had been an item on the news about the number of stray dogs. Tom had always thought every dog already had an owner to look after it. Now he realized there were thousands of poor, homeless, miserable dogs wandering about, and he just knew that he would have to rescue one from its awful lonely life and give it a good home. The programme said that stray dogs were all over the place. All Tom had to do was find one. He didn't need biscuit tins or carrots or anything.

Tom looked eagerly up and down his short road. There was not a dog in sight. He began to walk towards the shops a couple of streets away, carefully looking everywhere for a dog that might need rescuing.

He tried giving a high whistle. Dogs always answered whistles. Tom had only recently been taught by Jane how to do the wolf-whistle that men give to beautiful girls. Jane had told Tom it was the same as an owl's call and Tom liked to think he could whistle like an owl. He wasn't sure if a dog would answer. Anyway, it was worth trying. He whistled several times.

There was a little old lady walking in front of him and she stopped and turned round. For some reason she seemed to be angry as she peered at Tom through her spectacles.

'Are you trying to be cheeky?' she demanded. Tom was most surprised. His mouth fell open and he shook his head. The old lady sniffed and carried on walking. Tom wondered what it was all about, shrugged his shoulders and whistled again. Instantly the old lady swung round, red-faced and swinging her handbag like a Viking's axe.

'I knew it!' she cried. 'It is you, you cheeky young good-for-nothing. Your mother ought to box your ears for whistling like that at old ladies.'

'It's an owl call!' explained Tom in a whisper.

'Owl! Don't give me any of your nonsense. You ought to be ashamed of yourself. You're just a young . . .'

Tom wasn't listening any longer. He had

spotted a dog. He nipped round the old lady and ran after the hound, which was quietly trotting towards the shops.

'Here, boy,' Tom called after the small black-and-white collie. 'Here, boy. Come here.' The dog stopped and watched Tom with a pair of bright black eyes. Tom ran straight up and began to pat the dog, feeling for its collar. It hadn't got one. That, thought Tom, must mean it's a stray.

'Are you a stray?' asked Tom, looking to see if it seemed worn-out, moth-eaten and in need of a good home.

The dog cocked one ear and looked at Tom with sad eyes. Tom nodded. 'I thought so. I could tell as soon as I saw you. Well, don't worry. I'm going to look after you. I'm Tom.' The dog put one forepaw against Tom's thigh. He was delighted. 'You come with me and everything will be all right.'

Tom began to walk back home, but the dog stayed right where it was. Tom went back and tried to pick it up. The collie's back end dangled down on one side and its front end on the other.

Tom struggled a few steps and then the

collie rolled lightly out of his arms and stood on the pavement, looking at Tom as if it wondered what game they were going to play next.

'Come on,' said Tom impatiently. But the dog would not budge. Stupid thing. You'd think it would come when it was being taken to a good home and good food, thought Tom. That gave him an idea. 'You stay there!' he shouted to the collie. 'Don't move until I get back!' He dashed home and burst into the house.

'Mum! Mum!' There was no answer. He called out into the back garden, but she wasn't there either. 'Where's Mum?' he shouted up the stairs. Jane shouted back from her bedroom.

'Over the road having coffee with Mrs Roberts.'

'Well, what do you think dogs like to eat?' cried Tom.

'Blue whales,' came the loud reply.

'No. I mean it,' said Tom. 'What do they really like?'

'Boa constrictors. They like dogs. They like dogs for breakfast,' said Jane. 'And lunch,' she added. 'And supper,' she called down.

'No!' screamed Tom in great distress.
The collie might have given up waiting and
wandered off by now. 'No, really, really?'

'Dog-food, meat, sausages, liver, bones ...'
said Jane. 'And stop shouting, you'll wake the
baby.'

What baby? They hadn't got a baby. His
sister really was horrible. He stormed into
the kitchen and flung open a cupboard.
There was nothing there. He searched the
fridge. Ah! A packet of mince. Just what he
needed. Tom hesitated for a moment. What
would Mum say? He had wanted to ask her.
It wasn't his fault if she was out. A dog's life
was at stake. It was an emergency. He seized
the mince and tore out of the house, leaping
over the low garden wall and skidding on to
the pavement.

The collie was still there, quietly sitting
beside a hedge and watching people and cars
as they passed by. Tom squealed to a halt
and the dog wagged its tail in greeting.
'Good dog. You are a good dog, aren't you?
Yes, you are.'

The collie was very interested in the

exciting smell that came from Tom's packet. The dog kept poking its nose against the paper and sniffing loudly. Tom grinned. 'Oh yes. You know what's in there, don't you? Dinner. Come on.' Tom pulled off a small lump of mince and laid it just in front of the collie's wet nose. The dog took one sniff and the mince disappeared. Tom beamed with pleasure. The dog might be greedy, but at least it didn't squeeze the mince to death before it fed.

Tom backed away, laying a trail of mince along the street. He could see the collie following a little way off, trotting from one mince-heap to the next. Tom's heart beat loudly. His plan was going to succeed. He hurried on in front of the dog all the way to the garden. There he put down the final lump of mince and hid behind a hedge.

At that moment a big black labrador wandered in and began sniffing the meat. 'Go away!' hissed Tom, and just then the collie trotted in, saw the labrador sniffing his mince and growled angrily. The ruff on the collie's neck bristled. The large labrador turned to face his enemy and almost tripped over a small dachshund, also on his way to the mince.

'Shoo!' cried Tom desperately, waving his arms at the two intruders. But the dogs took no notice.

Before any of them got to the mince, a sheep-dog came bounding into the garden, closely followed by three mongrels, a poodle, a terrier and a pair of very large, hairy Afghan hounds. Then they began to bark and growl. The noise was appalling. Tom covered his ears. By this time he was scared. He didn't know what to do.

The dogs were beginning to fight over the last pile of mince. They were leaping and snapping and yapping. The front door opened and Mum looked out to see what all the fuss was about. Tom saw one of the Afghans leap joyfully towards her. He closed his eyes as well as his ears.

For the next five minutes there was chaos. The dogs poured into the house, knocking Mum flying. They cannoned upstairs and downstairs, absolutely everywhere, barking all the time. Even with his ears tight shut, Tom heard Jane scream as her bedroom was suddenly invaded by a pack of excited dogs. A poodle skidded across her picture and the labrador tried to use her bed as a trampoline. Then they all tore back downstairs, woofing with delight.

They joined the other dogs in a mad dance around the dining-room table. Chairs toppled and crashed to the floor. The newspaper went flying and was quickly torn into whirling scraps of litter as forty-four paws shredded it in less than ten seconds. Then Mum shouted 'OUT!' at the top of her voice and, as if by magic, the dogs pounded out of the front door, laughing in a loud and doggy way. Silence slowly settled.

Mum collapsed into the nearest armchair. Tom came creeping in from the garden. He began to tiptoe upstairs.

'Tom!' Mum had seen him. He came back down.

'Tom, what do you know about all those dogs?' demanded Mum wearily.

'I . . .' began Tom. He found this question difficult to answer. 'I, I only asked the collie. He was the only one that was invited,' said Tom lamely.

Mum raised her hands in despair as she looked round the war-torn room. 'Why did they come here in the first place?' Tom bit his lip, then told her the whole story. When he had finished Mum nodded slowly and scratched her forehead.

At last she said, 'Mince is for people, not dogs. I know you would have asked if I'd been here, but you should have waited. I think you'd better buy some more mince with your pocket-money.' Tom nodded. Mum went to the kitchen to make a cup of tea before she began clearing up the mess.

'And, Tom,' she called out. 'I could never make up my mind if I liked dogs or not. Now I know that I don't, not even a little bit. Please don't bring any more dogs into the house.'

Tom went upstairs and lay on his bed. No rabbit, no dog, no pet. He was puzzled. He still could not understand why that old lady had got so cross with him.

3 Fox, or Monster?

Tom was busy exploring the small woods on the hilltop when he first saw the hole. It was a small hole, rather sandy around the edges. It was too large to be a rabbit hole, thought Tom. It must be a fox hole. Now, a fox would make a really good pet. They were almost like dogs, thought Tom, only their snouts were longer. A fox would make an unusual pet too. Even Jane would be impressed.

Tom lay on the ground and inspected the dark hole. He couldn't see a thing and he wondered how the fox could possibly see what it was doing. It ought to have a torch and helmet like the ones potholers wear to explore caves. Tom was going to put his hand down the hole to feel around, but then he thought the fox might be at home. He knew that he wouldn't like a giant hand thrust into his bedroom, so he supposed a fox would feel the same way. It might bite him. Anyway, all he had to do was wait for the fox to come out and catch it.

Dad had some netting in the garden. It had once covered the strawberries, before the birds got them, but now it was lying unwanted in the shed. As he rummaged beneath all the bean poles, Jane wandered over to see what her brother was up to.

'You can't have that,' she said helpfully. 'Dad will be furious.'

'Can't have what?' asked Tom. He hadn't taken anything yet.

'That,' said Jane.

'I haven't got anything,' said Tom indignantly.

'Well, what are you doing anyway?'

'Nothing to do with you.'

'Oh go on, tell me.' Jane was rather bored and she hoped that Tom was doing something interesting. Tom stopped searching the shed and he sat down on the step.

'I'm going to catch a fox,' he announced.
Jane began to giggle.

'You can't catch a fox,' she said at last.

'Why not?' Tom demanded.

'Where will you catch one?'

'Up on the hill, near the wood,' said Tom.

'There isn't a fox up there.'

'Yes there is. I saw it this morning.'

'You can't have done,' Jane said. 'Foxes
sleep during the day, so there!'

Tom wondered why his sister always knew
more than he did. It was most annoying.
'Well, I saw its hole,' he said, 'and sooner or
later it will come out of its hole and I shall be
there with my net and . . .'

'The fox will jump up and bite you,'
interrupted Jane. 'You're mad.'

'You're a coward! I'm not afraid of foxes,'
Tom shouted back.

'You still won't catch it,' Jane insisted.
'Foxes only come out at night!'

Tom stormed into the garden shed and
cried, 'We'll see about that!' Jane wandered
off and Tom at last found all the netting he
needed. Then he returned to the fox hole.

He sat there patiently with the net across

his knees, ready to throw it over the fox the moment it poked its nose out. Tom's eyes hardly moved from just above the hole. After ten minutes his arms ached. He began to wonder if Jane was right after all. He decided to try and wake the fox up and frighten it out of its den and into his net.

First of all he jumped up and down on what he imagined to be the roof of the den. Nothing came out. Then he put his face as close to the hole as he dared and shouted down it twice, very quickly, in case the fox came shooting out and biffed him. Nothing came out. He found an old fencing stake and pushed and poked that down into the hole and prodded around with it, yelling at the same time. There was a slight movement at the hole's entrance and a large brown earwig slowly crawled out into a patch of sunlight. Tom sighed, picked up his net and trudged home. It was getting near teatime.

While Jane was out of the room Tom asked Mum about foxes. 'When do they sleep?'

'During the day. They usually come out at night,' said Mum.

'Why does Jane always know more than I do?'

'You'll catch up with her. She's had three more years of learning, remember.'

'Well, I think children should be told about foxes before they're eight,' said Tom.

'What use would that be?' asked Mum. Tom was quiet for a moment.

'It would help,' he said at last. He didn't want to tell Mum about his plans.

Jane came bounding into the room. Tom sighed. He knew what was coming. 'Well,' she said, 'where is it? Where's the fox?'

'What fox?' asked Mum. 'Why is everybody going on about foxes?'

'Tom's going to catch a fox and train it to jump through hoops of fire and fetch his slippers and catch robbers.'

'No I'm not!' cried Tom.

'Really, Jane, you do make up some stories,' Mum said.

Jane started eating a sandwich. As soon as Mum's back was turned she leaned across the table and whispered to Tom, 'Where is it?' Tom stuck out his tongue. Then he noticed that Mum was watching, so he pretended he was searching for a crumb stuck on the tip of his nose. Mum raised her eyebrows, but she didn't say anything.

Tom lay awake thinking. If foxes only came out at night then he would just have to go out at night to catch one. Mum and Dad were still up, watching a film.

Tom stared into the darkness beyond the bedroom window. He couldn't see the hill, but he could see how dark and quiet it was. There were probably hundreds of foxes roaming around out there, he thought. He heard his parents coming upstairs and dashed back into bed. While they had a bath, he lay in bed and carefully thought out his plans. It was a fine night. He knew where Dad's big torch was and the net he'd found that afternoon. That was all he needed. Oh, and a heavy stick, just in case. Or maybe he could borrow the bread knife.

Tom waited until Mum and Dad had gone to bed and the house went quiet. He got up, dressed and crept downstairs. He felt wide awake as he put on his anorak and found the torch. Very quietly he let himself out through the kitchen door. He was about to shut it when he realized that he had forgotten the bread knife in his excitement. He quickly fetched it and set off.

It was very dark and a little cold. There were too many clouds for the moon to show much light. Tom didn't like to switch on the torch until he was well away from the houses. He walked silently up the lane towards the hill that rose black and gloomy in front. He was just about to switch on the torch when a weird loud noise, right in his ear, made him drop the torch with a clatter. There was a fearful slobbering noise from behind the hedge and a rustling of leaves as if something enormous was forcing its way through. Terror filled Tom's heart.

He fell to his knees in his frantic efforts to find the torch, which had rolled to one side.

At last he put one hand on it. The rustling was getting louder and he could hear heavy, raspy breathing. Tom turned the torch towards the hedge and switched it on. Nothing happened. Not a flicker. Something had broken when Tom dropped it. Now he was so scared he could hardly move. All the time he could hear the enormous unknown creature blundering wildly against the hedge, as if to burst through at any moment.

Tom began to tiptoe back towards the house. The rustling and breathing followed. Tom walked faster. The monster still kept up with him, wheezing and clattering against the stiff branches. Tom gripped the handle of the bread knife fiercely, although he was certain the monster was far too large to be scared by a bread knife. Certainly Tom was scared of *it*. He walked faster and faster until he was running in his panic. The monster still lumbered on behind, getting louder and louder. It seemed miles to safety. He was panting and almost crying with fear.

At last he reached the house. He dashed upstairs and flung himself into bed. It took ten minutes to get his breath back, and even then he was still trembling. He fell asleep.

Mum found him like that in the morning – lying in bed with his anorak still on, clutching a bread knife in one hand and a broken torch in the other.

'Whatever have you been up to?' she asked in amazement.

'I thought I saw a monster,' explained Tom, and that was all he would say.

He went back to the lane in bright daylight to see if the monster was still there. Tom peered cautiously over the hedge. Yes, it was, and as soon as the monster saw Tom it hurried over and put its own large head over the hedge.

It was a horse.

4 A Souvenir from the Zoo

Dad took a day off work. Mum thought
that if they all went to the zoo, perhaps Tom
would see enough to satisfy his need for a
pet. Certainly Tom and Jane were excited
by the idea.

'We haven't been to the zoo for ages,' Jane
said. 'Do you remember the last time we
went, Dad? The monkeys thought Tom was
one of them and they tried to pull him into
their cage!' Tom went bright red.

'They didn't!' he said hotly, and he
hurried upstairs to get his duffle-bag. It was
true though. On their last visit Tom had
stood against the monkey cage so that Dad
could take a photograph. One of the

monkeys had slipped a long hairy arm
through the bars and grabbed a handful
of Tom's hair. He had felt very foolish. Of
course Jane thought it was the best photo
in the album.

It was a warm day and Mum and Dad
had made a picnic lunch. They all piled into
the car. Nicola and her brother Paul called
out from over the road to ask where they
were going. Jane leaned out of the car
window and shouted back.

'We won't be long. We're just taking Tom
back to the zoo. The monkeys have asked if
they can have him back.'

'Jane! Don't shout like that,' said Dad.
'Pull your head in before it gets knocked off.'

'I'll knock it off,' murmured Tom. Mum
turned round.

'Now look, you two, we're going to enjoy
ourselves, so we'll have none of that.'

Jane looked at Tom and Tom looked at
Jane. They both raised their eyebrows as if
they were terribly surprised Mum should
think they would ever quarrel with each
other. They settled down and watched the
traffic until they reached the zoo. Once the

car was parked, they rushed off, trying to see everything at once.

Jane took great delight in showing Tom a fat boa constrictor snoozing in the reptile house. The snake was curled round a lump of dead wood.

'It's probably just eaten,' said Jane. 'I expect it swallowed the keeper.'

'I bet they haven't got a blue whale here,' Tom said. Jane giggled and approached the keeper on duty.

'Excuse me, but is there a blue whale here at all?' Jane tried to look angelic. The keeper smiled and shook his head.

'No, miss. I'm sorry. We haven't got a blue whale. Bit too big, you see.'

Jane seemed disappointed. 'Oh dear. I wanted to show my brother. Well, have you got a green whale?'

'Green whale?' The keeper frowned. He didn't know whether or not Jane was pulling his leg.

'Or a pink one with purple spots?' suggested Jane, but she could not keep a straight face any longer and she began to laugh. Tom wished Jane would not do such awful things, but he could not help laughing all the same. The keeper sighed heavily and walked off, trying to look important.

Mum and Dad caught up with them and they decided to eat. Mum and Dad were both rather tired and they sat on the grass among the cages after lunch and told the children they could look round by themselves.

'But don't go too far away,' warned Mum.

At first they went around together, returning every now and then to tell Mum and Dad excitedly of their latest finds. But Mum and Dad soon fell asleep and Tom and Jane quarrelled. Tom went off in a huff to explore for himself.

He passed by the penguin pool and stopped for a moment to watch them being fed. His eye was caught by a rather small, seedy-looking bird that stood by itself in one corner. The keeper threw some fish into the pool and soon the fish had all gone. Only Tom noticed that the small lonely penguin had not eaten a scrap. His heart was filled with pity for it. It must have been abandoned by the other penguins. Tom went round to where the poor penguin stood moping beside a low wall.

He leaned over and talked softly to the bird. 'You poor thing. Haven't you got any friends? Neither have I. Don't you like fish? Neither do I – unless they're fish fingers. I don't suppose they give you fish fingers here, do they?' The little bird did not seem to be very interested in Tom's chatter. It just stood there looking very sorry for itself. Tom wished he could do something to help it.

The keepers left the penguins and went to bath the elephants. The crowd followed. This gave Tom his chance. He was surprised how easy it was to catch a penguin. After all the difficulty he'd had in the past, he was sure this one would kick up a fuss too. He leaned over the wall, put both arms carefully round the bird, which didn't even struggle, and slipped it into his duffle-bag. Then he walked quickly away.

Jane was already back with Mum and Dad and they were wondering what had happened to Tom when he arrived, carefully carrying his bag. It was time to go, Mum said. She handed a pile of uneaten picnic food to Tom and told him to put it in his bag.

'Come on, Tom, hurry up,' said Dad. Tom seemed to be taking an awfully long time. He was putting the food in with great care, keeping one hand over the top of the bag, just in case the penguin decided to fly out. Tom could not remember if penguins could fly or not.

'Buck up, Tom!' moaned Mum.

'He's probably got something in there,' joked Jane. 'He's probably got a baby camel or a boa constrictor in there. You know he wants a pet.'

Tom glared at her and told her to be quiet. He slung the bag over his shoulder just to prove she was wrong. There was a small squeak from deep inside. Luckily nobody heard.

The journey home seemed to last an age. Tom sat quite still, nursing the duffle-bag on his lap, hoping the penguin would not choose this time to start wriggling or squawking.

'Can I have another sandwich?' asked Jane, halfway home.

'They're in Tom's bag,' Mum said.

Jane leaned over and started to fiddle with the top of the bag. Tom snatched it back, shouting angrily. 'Leave it alone!'

'She only wants a sandwich,' said Dad.

'I'll get it out then.'

'But you don't know what kind I want,' Jane complained.

'I'll get it out,' insisted Tom. Mum sighed.

'Tell him what kind you want and let him get it for you.'

'I want a cucumber one with no salt or pepper on it,' Jane said.

Tom slid his hand into the bag, keeping the top shut, while Jane stared at him in the most odd way. He felt the penguin soft and warm against his hand. Then he found the sandwiches. By good luck he pulled out a cucumber sandwich first time. Jane looked at it in disgust.

'It's been pecked!' she cried. 'What have you got in there – an ostrich?'

'Don't be stupid, Jane,' said Mum. 'Just get on and eat it.'

The penguin seemed rather upset by Jane's voice, because it began to squeak. Not very loudly, but loud enough to be heard by everybody. Dad was slowing down behind a lorry.

'Brakes have started squeaking,' he growled.

'You'll have to oil them, Dad,' suggested Jane. Tom pulled a face.

'You can't oil brakes, stupid. Then they wouldn't work at all.' Dad laughed and said Tom was right. The penguin was quiet after that.

When they got home Tom said he was worn out. Mum suggested an early bed, so Tom crept upstairs, taking the duffle-bag with him. Mum wondered why he wanted all those old sandwiches, but she was too tired to say anything and she soon forgot about it. In fact she dozed off and didn't wake until Dad brought her a cup of tea at half past nine.

'Why don't you have a bath and go to bed?' he said. 'You look worn out.'

Mum nodded and drank her tea. She went upstairs to run a bath. As she passed Tom's room she was surprised to hear him talking.

'That's right,' he was saying. 'You settle yourself down and we'll soon have you looking better. A nice bit of salmon sandwich – I expect you'll like that. Shall I tell you a story? How about *Jack and the Beanstalk*. Once upon a time there was a poor boy called ...'

Mum pushed open the door and looked in. Tom was sitting up in bed. At the other end of the bed, also sitting up, was a penguin, carefully preening its feathers. 'Tom! Dad!' screamed Mum. Dad came pounding up.

'Tom! What are you doing? Where did that penguin come from?'

'*Sssh!*' hissed Tom. 'I was just going to tell it a story.'

But Mum and Dad did not want to hear about Jack and the beanstalk. They wanted to know about the penguin, and Tom had to to tell them. As soon as he'd finished, Dad went to the telephone and rang the zoo. They were rather surprised to hear Dad's news and they promised to come and pick up the penguin in the morning. Dad explained to Tom how wrong it was to take penguins, even if Tom thought he was doing a good deed. Tom sighed and went to sleep, and the penguin spent that night in the bath with a tin of sardines that Mum had found in the kitchen.

Mum and Dad went to bed. 'What are we going to do?' asked Dad. 'Tom's determined to get an animal into this house.' Mum lay thinking for a moment. Then she smiled.

'I wouldn't worry. I expect he'll forget all about it soon. Then it will be something else. What he really needs is a friend of his own age. Even a penguin is not much good for playing football with.' Dad tried to smile.

'I only hope you're right,' he said.

5 A Rather Large Pet

Tom pushed his hand in amongst the cereal, trying to find the free plastic dinosaur. Jane watched him for a moment and then asked Mum, 'What do you think is the best animal in the world, Mum?'

'I think people are nice,' said Mum. Jane jumped down from her seat excitedly.

'Hey, Tom!' she cried. 'You could have a person and build a cage for it and feed it carrots through the bars and take it for walks!'

Tom hardly looked up from the cereal packet. 'You're nuts,' he said.

'Look, here it is.' He held up a small yellow diplodocus. He stood it on the table. The diplodocus slowly toppled over.

'It's dead!' cried Jane. 'It's eaten too much cereal. I'm not surprised it died. It was probably poisoned. I don't know how you eat that stuff, it's yucky. Look at that mouldy dinosaur. It's gone all yellow with the lurgy. It's got yellow fever. I bet it died in agony . . .'

'Jane!' said Mum sharply. 'For goodness sake. We're trying to have breakfast.' Tom at last managed to get the dinosaur to stand up.

'There are five more of these to collect,' he hinted and he looked hard at Mum.

'If you think I'm going out to buy five more packets so that you can get plastic monsters you'd better think again.'

'You'll be poisoned like that dinosaur,' added Jane.

Tom finished breakfast and went off by himself, as usual. He was still on the lookout for a pet. He didn't mind what it was, so long as it was warm and friendly.

He wandered slowly away from the road and into the fields, not stopping until he saw an old, grey donkey standing in the long thistled grass of one small field. He had never seen it before. Tom didn't know anybody who had a donkey. Where had it come from?

The donkey lifted its head and eyed Tom carefully as he approached. Then it carried on munching.

'Hello!' said Tom. 'Who are you?' He stretched out one hand and gently patted the donkey. Once more the animal lifted its big head and gazed at Tom thoughtfully. It flicked its ears several times. Tom picked it some grass to eat. The donkey sniffed the grass and then looked at Tom, as if to say, 'Why bother to pick it? There's plenty on the ground.'

'I think you're lovely,' Tom said, stroking the old grey head.

He left the donkey standing in the field and wandered off. Sometimes he glanced back at the lonely grey figure. At last he stopped and sat down. Tom was now some distance away, but he could still clearly see the animal. The donkey did look sad in that field by itself. Surely it could not belong to anybody? It must have strayed into the field while it was searching for a kind new owner.

All the same, Tom wasn't sure. He knew he mustn't take things that belonged to other people. He wondered what Mum and Dad

would think about having a donkey in the
house, or at any rate in the garden, especially
so soon after the penguin. On the other
hand, Mum had always said he must be kind
to animals.

Tom decided to wait and see if anybody
came to look after the donkey. He waited
and waited, wandering about in the sun,
swishing at the grass with a thin stick. A
whole hour passed on his new watch, but
nobody appeared. Tom felt sure that the
donkey had been thrown out of its home by
some cruel master who thought it was too old
for work.

A second hour passed and still no one
came. Tom was certain now. The donkey
obviously had no owner. Unfortunately it
was time for lunch so he would have to go
home before he could do anything to rescue
the poor creature.

'Have you been trying to catch people?'
asked Jane at lunch.

'Yes, and I caught one too,' answered
Tom at once.

'Where is it?' asked Jane.

'I put it under a flower pot.'

'It must have been a gigantic flower pot.'

'It was,' replied Tom. 'It was as large as Dad.'

'What on earth are you two talking about?' asked Mum. That made them both go quiet.

When lunch was finished Tom went straight to the garden shed and hunted around for an old bit of rope. He found some thick string, wound round some beansticks. So he unwound it and was surprised when all the beansticks fell across the shed floor. He hurried off to the field.

The donkey was still there, chewing the grass, swishing his tail this way and that in a rather bored fashion. Tom ran over.

'Hello!' he cried. 'I'm back!' The donkey took little notice. 'I've come to save you,' Tom said grandly. 'You'll soon have a marvellous home and I'll feed you the best food there is,' he added, wondering what donkeys ate besides grass.

Tom stood back and looked at the donkey and wondered how exactly he could get the animal home. The best way would be to ride him. From a distance a donkey looks easy to ride, but when Tom stood right next to the animal he realized that it was very large. However, he was not going to be put off.

He grabbed the donkey's mane with one hand and tried to haul himself up, with no success. The donkey was so fat! Its sides seemed to stick out everywhere. The animal was really the most awkward shape. Tom tried again and again, but he couldn't get anywhere. He wished he had a friend to help him up.

Eventually Tom got the donkey to move over next to the fence. He climbed on to the fence and waited. The beast would not come quite close enough. Why didn't it understand that Tom was trying to save it! At last it took two steps closer to the fence. Tom grinned and stretched out one leg. There, he was astride the animal.

The donkey wasn't used to a strange

weight on its back and took a step forward.
The round fat body seemed to shift sideways
beneath Tom and he found himself lying in a
heap on the grass, quite breathless. The
donkey gazed calmly down at Tom. It let out
a great sigh.

Tom did not give up. He suddenly
remembered the rope and placed it round
the donkey's neck. 'Right,' said Tom firmly.
'You're going to come with me.' The donkey
was so surprised that it followed Tom as he
led the way out of the field and towards the
house.

As they approached the garden Tom
began to wonder what everybody would
say when they saw his marvellous pet. He
decided to put the beast in the garden for the
time being. He tied it safely to a small bush.
Then he went indoors to try and find it some
food. He also thought about telling Mum if
she seemed in the right mood. There was
no point in bothering her if she wasn't.

Tom could not find any food. Before he
could go back outside, Mum grabbed him
and said that she had almost forgotten about
his dentist's appointment. There was just

time to go. Tom started to tell Mum about the donkey, then he decided it was definitely the wrong moment. Anyway, the donkey would be all right. It was quite safe in the garden.

The dentist took a long time. When at last Mum and Tom got home they heard peculiar loud noises coming from the back garden. A strange and dreadful sight met their eyes. Dad and Jane were desperately chasing the old grey donkey. It was galloping madly about the garden, tossing its big grey head and braying noisily. A small bush dangled from its neck, torn up by the roots. All over the garden Tom could see the mess its hard, kicking feet had caused. The fence was smashed in three places. The vegetable patch looked like a muddy brown and green stew. The grass was covered with deep hoof marks.

Mum and Tom joined in the chase. When the animal saw Tom it stopped long enough for Dad to grab the rope. Everybody started to ask where had it come from? Nobody knew, though they all looked at Tom very hard. Tom went red and said that he thought, but wasn't sure, that he'd seen it in the small field up the road. But how had it got into the garden? Everybody looked at Tom again, but Mum said he'd just been to the dentist. Tom decided to keep quiet for the time being.

Dad led the donkey back to the field, with the help of a few mashed vegetables. When he returned he set about clearing up the garden. He mended the fence and replanted what tatty vegetables were left. During tea, Tom said that large pets were probably more trouble than they were worth. Small animals were definitely better, he said. Mum and Dad looked at each other and wondered if Tom knew something about the donkey after all. Then they shook their heads. No. Tom was too young to handle a donkey, wasn't he?

6 A Duck and a Ducking

Jane rushed down the stairs two at a time.

'Jane!' shouted Dad. 'Do you have to make that noise?'

'Sorry!' cried Jane as she reached the front door.

'Where are you off to now?' asked Dad. He was helping Tom with a jigsaw in the front room.

'Just to the pond. Nicola says there are ducks down there.' Tom stopped and looked up at his sister.

'Ducks?'

'Yes, ducks. Hundreds and hundreds of ducks,' said Jane. 'The whole pond is covered with them. You can't see the water at all. You wouldn't even guess there was a pond underneath because some of the ducks even have to sit on top of the other . . .'

'Jane, that's enough,' said Dad. 'You really do tell the most awful stories.'

'Well, that's what Nicola said anyway,' insisted Jane.

'What kind of ducks are they?' asked Tom.

'Cheerio!' cried Jane as she ran out, slamming the door behind her. Dad frowned.

Tom put down the piece of puzzle he'd been trying to fit and asked, 'Do you think ducks like people, Dad?'

'If they're kind to them.' Dad looked hard at Tom. 'I don't expect they make very good pets though. They're a bit wet and flappy.'

But Tom didn't hear. He was already thinking about pet ducks. He gave up doing the puzzle and went down to the pond to see things for himself. Jane was still there, with Nicola and Paul. Paul was the same age as Tom, but he was in a different class at school. The two boys never talked to each other. Neither of them knew why, especially as they lived so close together. As their sisters

were best friends, it just seemed right that
Paul and Tom should think of each other as
enemies.

Tom stared at the shiny surface of the
pond. It was true. There were ducks – or
rather there was one. That wasn't nearly as
many as Jane had said. Tom only wanted
one pet though and it looked like a very nice
duck. It was black with white sides and it
kept diving and popping up somewhere else.
Tom was already thinking how he could
catch it.

'Mind you don't fall in!' Jane yelled from
the other side, and Tom heard the other two
laughing. He went red. What kind of baby
did they think he was? He watched the duck
for a few more moments and then went back
home. He needed some duck-catching

equipment and he thought his old seaside shrimping net would be best. Just as he set off back to the pond Jane came in.

'Ah!' she said. 'Aha! I bet you're going to try and catch that duck.'

'No,' said Tom angrily. 'Why should I?'

'Because you're mad of course. Nicola thinks you're barmy trying to get a pet. She says you can have Paul any day. She says he eats porridge and likes to be taken for a walk once a week.'

Tom made a rude face at his sister and marched off to the pond with his net. The duck was still diving down and popping up, and Nicola's brother Paul was sitting by the edge. Tom approached warily. Paul watched him without saying a word. Tom slowly pushed his net towards the duck, which kept out of the way. He whistled his owl call and shouted and waved, but the duck came no nearer.

'It can't hear you,' said Paul suddenly. 'Its ears will be full of water from all that diving, you see. Are you going to catch it?' Tom nodded. 'Are you going to cook it?' asked Paul.

'No! I'm going to tame it and teach it to do tricks,' boasted Tom.

'Like what?'

'Well, I shall teach it to dive really deep and look for sunken treasure and things and then it can bring the treasure back to me.'

'You'll never do that!' said Paul, wishing that he'd thought of it. Then he said, 'Did you really bring a penguin home from the zoo in your duffle-bag? Nicola says you did, but I don't believe her because she's always teasing me.'

Tom grinned. 'Yes,' he said, stirring the pond with his net. 'I really did.'

'How did you do it?' asked Paul eagerly. Tom shrugged his shoulders.

'I just picked it up. It wasn't a very big one and I brought it home, but Mum and Dad found it and it was taken back. You know what they're like.' Paul groaned in sympathy.

'How are we going to get this duck?' asked Paul. Tom didn't know. Paul said, 'Suppose I go round the other side and shoo it over to you. You could hide in that big bush and when it comes close enough . . . swoosh!'

Tom grinned. 'That might work. How will you shoo it over?'

'I thought I could sort of throw a few stones towards it – only small ones.'

'Be careful you don't hit it.'

'Don't worry. I'm a dead shot. I'll miss it all right.'

Paul ran round to the other side. Tom carefully hid himself in the branches of the bush that overhung the pond.

Paul picked up a few small stones and began to lob them towards the duck. Splot! Plob! The duck seemed a bit surprised at this bombing and it moved slowly away from the falling pebbles. Tom gripped the net harder. More stones fell from the sky and the worried duck slowly moved closer and closer to the shelter of the bush. Tom wished his heart wouldn't beat so loudly. The duck was sure to hear it throbbing away.

Paul was certainly doing his job well. The duck came even closer. Tom pushed the net towards it. The duck stopped and circled, just out of reach. Tom shifted forward and felt the branches tremble beneath his weight. The net was almost over the duck.

The sly bird must have seen the net from the corner of its eye. It suddenly flapped its wings in alarm, squawked and kicked up a spray of water as it took to the air. Tom lunged forward, missed and felt himself slip. He dropped the net and grabbed a branch. There was a tremendous splash as his feet and legs plunged into the cold water. He was left dangling, half in and half out, thrashing his legs helplessly and hanging on to the branch for dear life.

'Hold on!' shouted Paul as he raced round from the other side of the pond.

He climbed into the bush and reached out for Tom's hands. 'I'll pull you back!' he said breathlessly. Paul slid out further and wrapped his fingers round one of Tom's wrists. He tried to balance himself in the branches, but they were thin and whippy. 'Hang on,' said Paul. 'I need a better grip.' He moved forward again and then the branch that held him up simply snapped off under the strain of two bodies.

They both fell into the pond, yelling and splashing. They came up standing firmly on the bottom, but wet through. Paul had pieces of water weed draped over his head and face. The two gasping boys waded to the bank and sat down to get their breath back. Then Tom noticed Paul's water-weed hat and began to laugh. They both laughed even more when the black and white duck circled low over the pond and then slapped down on the middle of the water as if nothing had happened.

The boys went home to find some dry clothes. They also found two jeering sisters and two angry mothers who put them straight to bed, just in case. Tom's father was hopping mad.

'He might have drowned!' he said to Mum later on.

'The pond's not deep enough for that,' said Mum. 'Anyway, he was bound to fall in sooner or later. I doubt if it will happen again. He was quite frightened really. It's a good thing Paul was with him.'

As soon as Paul's mum let him get up, he came over to see Tom. 'Shall we try and get the duck again?' Tom shook his head.

'No. The trouble with animals is that they never do what you want them to.'

'I know,' agreed Paul. 'My rabbit's like

that. I tried to teach him to walk a tightrope, but all he did was sit and scratch himself and wriggle his nose.'

'What are we going to do then?' asked Tom.

Paul thought for a while. 'I know where there's a camp,' he suggested.

'A camp!' said Tom excitedly.

'Well, it's not exactly a camp yet, but it will be when I've finished building it and then I'm going to have secret meetings,' explained Paul.

'Who with?'

Paul laughed. 'You of course, dope! And sisters can't come,' he added.

'You bet,' agreed Tom. The two boys set off for Paul's camp.

'Where are you two going?' called Jane and Nicola from over the road.

Tom looked at Paul and Paul looked at Tom. They didn't say a word. They just marched off up the road and all Jane and Nicola heard was the sound of laughter.

7 The Camp

It was a very good place for a camp. It was
up in the wood, near the fox hole. Several
small trees grew close together and they had
branches low down. They were easy to
climb.

'We could use one as a lookout post,'
Tom suggested. Paul thought that was a
good idea. The two boys began to collect as
many long branches as they could find and
they stacked them around the tree trunks.
It began to get quite dark inside the camp.
Tom stamped down all the ferns that were
growing on their floor. It wasn't long before
the camp looked quite good. Paul walked
around the outside.

'We ought to camouflage it,' he said.

'What does that mean?' asked Tom.

'We ought to hide it so that Nicola and Jane don't know it's here.' Paul gathered some ferns and stuck them amongst the branches to look like leaves. 'That's better,' he said.

'I'm going to get a torch,' said Tom. 'I might be able to get a few biscuits as well, if Mum's in a good mood.'

At the end of the road Tom joined Paul. Paul had managed to get three and a half slices of cake from his mum. Nicola had secretly followed her brother, so now the two girls met each other and followed Tom and Paul together.

As the boys walked up the hill to the wood, Tom told Paul all about the monster horse that had frightened him a few nights earlier. Paul said he wouldn't have been frightened at all.

'I'm not scared of the dark,' he said.

'Neither am I,' declared Tom. 'It wasn't the dark that was scary – it was the noises.'

'I'm not scared of noises either,' said Paul.

Tom was quiet for a few moments. Then he suddenly leaped in front of Paul and screamed at his friend, 'YAAAAGH!!' Paul jumped in the air from fright and almost fell over.

'What are you doing?' he cried.

'You are scared of noises,' said Tom. 'It's because you don't expect it, you see.'

'I was surprised, that's all,' mumbled Paul.

They reached the camp. They didn't see Jane and Nicola hiding just a few trees away and smiling at one another and pointing at the secret camp. Tom and Paul knelt down and crept under the branches. The ferns they had used for camouflage were beginning to wilt and looked rather odd, but that didn't worry the boys. There was just enough room for them inside, and they sat like kings and slowly ate their biscuits and cake. Tom thought Paul's cake was a bit stale and Paul thought Tom's biscuits were a bit soggy. They were enjoying themselves.

Jane and Nicola crept away and talked about what they would do. Nicola suggested charging the camp and taking it over.

'No,' said Jane. 'Let's pretend we don't

know about it at all. When they've gone, we can do something to the camp and they'll wonder who it was.'

The two girls thought this was the best idea. After Tom and Paul had left their camp to go home for tea, the girls crept in and ate the rest of the cake and biscuits.

The next morning the boys went straight to the camp after breakfast. They looked at the brown ferns on the walls and picked new ones from the floor of the camp. Tom climbed to the top of one tree. He stared across the fields. 'Paul! I can see Nicola and Jane coming this way! Quick!' Tom shot down the tree and the two boys huddled under the branches, holding their breath. Soon they saw the girls walking through the wood, coming straight towards them.

'Nicola,' said Jane in a loud voice. 'I think the boys have got a camp near here. Let's find it.'

'That's a good idea,' shouted Nicola. The boys looked at each other with round eyes. Tom put a finger to his lips and Paul nodded.

'I'm sure it's around here,' said Nicola.

She was standing right by the entrance to the camp. Paul could see her brown sandals and dirty socks. He wanted to bang her toes, but that would give them away.

'Have a good search,' Jane said and she came over. The girls wandered all round the camp pretending they could not see it. At last Jane said, 'I don't think it's here after all. Let's look somewhere else.' Jane and Nicola strolled off, laughing to themselves. Tom and Paul breathed a sigh.

'Phew! I thought they were going to find us,' said Paul.

'It's because of the camouflage,' said Tom. 'It was a good idea. Let's have the rest of the biscuits and cake.'

They searched and searched, but they could not find the food. Paul was sure he knew just where he had hidden it. They went home feeling very puzzled. It was a mystery. Tom told Dad about it.

'Maybe somebody else knows about your camp,' Dad said.

'It's camouflaged,' Tom answered.

'Oh. Perhaps an animal took your biscuits. A fox maybe?' Tom nodded. It could have been a fox. Jane giggled and had to hide her face.

In the afternoon the boys went back to the camp. The ferns had wilted again and they had to pick fresh ones from inside the camp. The floor was quite bare now. They sat down and sorted out what they had brought from their houses. Tom had two tomato sandwiches and Paul had five small apples. They ate the sandwiches and buried the apples carefully in one corner.

As soon as the boys left the camp, Jane and Nicola went in and ate all the apples. Then they ran home laughing. When Paul and Tom returned and found a hole in the ground and no apples, they were amazed.

'Foxes must be very clever,' said Tom.

'I didn't think foxes ate apples at all. I thought they ate rabbits.'

Tom grinned. 'Maybe they like a sort of apple sauce with their rabbit.'

The two boys laughed until Tom suddenly jumped up. 'Ouch!' he cried. 'Something bit me.' He scratched his leg. Paul leaped into the air.

'Ow! Something bit me!' He scratched at

his ankle. Tom looked at the ground and gasped.

'It's ants!' The floor was covered with masses of red ants where Tom and Paul had pulled up the last ferns. 'There must have been a nest under those ferns,' said Tom.

'This place is no good for a camp,' groaned Paul, still scratching. They sighed and hurried out of the camp, straight into Jane and Nicola.

'Aha!' cried Nicola. 'We've found your camp.'

'Now we know where it is, and you won't be able to stop us using it,' added Jane. Tom looked at Paul. They were both thinking the same thing. Jane peered inside the camp.

'Oh it's lovely!' she cried. 'I think this would make a smashing camp for you and me, Nicola.' Jane grinned at Tom. 'It was so kind of you to make it for us. Saves us all the hard work.'

Nicola tapped Jane on the shoulder and said, 'Mind you, I hear there's a funny animal that comes and steals their food.'

'Really?' cried Jane. 'How very strange.' Paul stepped forward.

'You can have the camp if you want it,' he said grandly. Jane's face fell. She had not expected that.

'Yes, it's yours,' said Tom. 'We don't want it any more.' The boys smiled at each other and walked off. Nicola and Jane watched them go. Jane shrugged her shoulders.

'Come on, they said we could have it,' she said. They crawled in and sat on the floor.

'I wonder why they don't – OUCH!' cried Nicola, jumping up and banging her head on the roof.

'Yow! Ow!' screamed Jane, and the two girls dashed out of the camp madly brushing the ants from their legs.

Tom and Paul were halfway down the hill, but they heard the yells and laughed. They were thinking of building another camp, one they would tell nobody about.

'There's still one thing I don't understand,' said Paul. 'I don't think a fox would eat cake, biscuits and apples. That's not right.' Tom thought for a while.

'It was those ants,' he said, and he nodded. 'Those ants found them and ate them.'

66

'What! All those apples and everything?'
cried Paul.

'There were a lot of ants,' said Tom. He
saw Jane and Nicola come out of the wood
still scratching themselves. 'Lots and lots,' he
said. 'Come on, let's see what we can get for
the new camp.'

Dogs Are Different

1 Geronimo!

It was almost Christmas and very cold. It had rained the whole day and Martin had been stuck indoors with not much to do and only his mother and older brother for company. Mum was OK, but Luke and Martin were always quarrelling these days and Martin reckoned he had suffered. He always seemed to come off worst.

He stared out through the wet window at grey streets, grey trees and a grey sky. Christmas. They had said on television it would not be a white one this year. That was obvious, thought Martin. It was going to be grey all over. He rolled off the chair and switched the TV on. Billiards, Test-Card,

Open University and cooking. What a great choice. Christmas was supposed to be the most exciting time of the year, all fun and games, laughter and colour. But not this year. It was going to be grey from start to finish.

Luke sauntered into the room, his hands deep in his pockets. He pushed the door open with his shoulder. 'What's on telly?'

'Nothing,' said Martin, turning back to the window sulkily.

'Don't be stupid. There must be something on. Look.' He switched the telly on again. 'See? Billiards, cooking – there's always something on, stupid.'

Martin ignored him. Luke was eleven, two years older than himself. They had never got on very well and since Mum had re-married a few months back, things had been worse. Luke was a niggler. He picked on Martin all day, arguing about little things – such little things that Martin was often driven to answering back simply because Luke's niggles were so petty. At least that was how it seemed to Martin.

Just to make matters worse, Luke didn't

like Roger. That was what their stepfather said they should call him – Roger. After all, he wasn't their real father, so they could hardly call him Dad. Martin liked that. He had never been allowed to call an adult by the first name before. He wanted to call his mother by her name too, but when he asked if he could, Mrs Ashley turned all red and said she would really rather he didn't. She preferred being called Mum.

Luke thought the whole thing was stupid. 'Roger is a stupid name and it's a stupid thing to do,' he sneered.

'I don't think so,' said Martin.

'You don't think at all,' said Luke, and he added 'creep' and went out.

After that Luke often called Martin 'Roger's little boy' and he made it sound the worst thing in the universe. Martin couldn't help it. He and Roger got on well, and that pleased his mother no end which made Luke even sulkier. Roger could see that Luke and Martin didn't get on together, but there wasn't much he could do about it. He usually just laughed and said everyone in this family was the same – Luke and Martin and their

mother. They all got too easily excited and
upset.

'Calm down,' he would say with a big
smile showing through his even bigger beard.
'Just calm down a bit and we'll sort things
out.' Well, sometimes it worked and peace
would return, but if it didn't then Roger just
went out for a long walk. Martin supposed
they were all meant to calm down while
Roger was out, or maybe Roger simply
didn't like listening to them shouting at each
other. Martin was used to it. He had grown
up with it.

But when he felt really bothered himself,
he tried to do what Roger suggested. He kept
quiet and let the others yell, while he slipped
into his own thoughts, a land of silent space
where only he could wander. It was a bit like
staring through a window at something you
didn't want to see and being able to pull the
curtains shut and blot it all out.

Martin began to wish he could shut all this
horrible rain out. Still, Christmas was
coming, with or without rain. He had no
idea what he was likely to get. He had got
presents for Mum and Roger, but hadn't

decided about Luke. The trouble was that every time they quarrelled he changed his mind. Sometimes he thought he would get Luke a secret codes kit and then they would argue and Martin would decide to buy him a deadly poisonous spider instead. But he had no idea about his own present.

'I know what I'm getting,' Luke had told him. 'A Walkman. But there's only one in the cupboard. I've seen it and it's got my name on it.'

This was the sort of moment when Martin had visions of Luke opening a large parcel that turned out to be a man-eating shark or better still, a Luke-eating shark. Martin fancied a Walkman for himself, but he put on a brave face. 'I don't mind.'

'You're green,' said Luke. 'You're green with envy. You've wanted one for years. Go on, admit it.' Martin had turned away and Luke went off laughing.

The back door slammed and Martin's attention wandered from the steady rain outside. There was a lot of noise from the kitchen. Martin couldn't make out what was going on and it sounded mysterious. He strained his ears and could just hear Roger's voice and Mum's voice talking loudly. There seemed to be a lot of scuffling going on and he thought Roger said, 'Hold it!' and then, 'Come here, you daft beggar.'

Martin went to the door and tried to go through to the kitchen, but it was jammed with something.

'Who is it?' shouted Roger.

'Me – Martin.'

'Don't come in.'

'Why not?'

'"Why not?" he says,' repeated Roger with a laugh.

'Go away!' shouted Mrs Ashley. 'You can't come in.'

Something crashed to the floor and chairs scraped on the lino.

'For Pete's sake, hold it!' hissed Roger.

'I can't. You hold her. She's too strong – oh!'

There was another crash and something broke. Roger and Mrs Ashley both began shouting at each other and the row went on. It sounded as if Godzilla had stumbled into their tiny kitchen and was thrashing about

on all sides. Martin pushed harder against
the door, but it wouldn't budge.

'Keep out!' yelled Roger.

A whole torrent of high-pitched barks
broke out. For a moment Martin stepped
back as if the door itself had growled at him.
Tremendous scurrying continued on the
other side, as if something big was racing
round and round the table, banging into
chairs and anything else in its path.

'It's no good trying to keep it a secret,' said
Mrs Ashley. 'Let Martin in.'

Something was moved away from the door
and Roger opened it, grinning from ear to
ear. Martin stepped wonderingly through.

'What's all the noi – oooff!!' Martin was
knocked completely off his feet as a young
Alsatian pup threw herself at him. At once

she began barking again, went off on another mad chase round the kitchen table, raced back to Martin who was trying to sit up, and pounced on him once more.

'I think she likes you.' Roger grinned.

Martin grabbed the energetic furball by the scruff and held her back. She stood there panting heavily, her bright eyes fixed on Martin and a long reddish-black tongue falling out of one side of her mouth.

'Where did she come from?' asked Martin incredulously.

Roger looked across at Mrs Ashley and she nodded. 'Well, I know it's not Christmas for another couple of days, but I had to collect her today. We were hoping to keep her a secret, but what with the barking and everything, I don't think there's going to much chance of that. It would be like trying to hide an earthquake.'

Mum folded her arms and gazed at Martin. 'What Roger is trying to tell you is that this is your Christmas present from the both of us. She's yours – and that means yours to feed, yours to walk and yours to train. Happy Christmas!'

Martin did not hear the last bit. He was still holding the Alsatian and staring at her. 'Mine?' he repeated.

'Yours,' said Roger and added a Happy Christmas too.

Martin looked at the puppy for a long time. She was a big dog already, with large pricked-up ears, a huge tail and great paddling paws. She was a lovely, soft, pale goldy-brown, with black ears and a few dark patches on her sides. She stuck out her nose and sniffed Martin's chin, giving it a quick lick.

'She's beautiful,' he murmured.

Mrs Ashley laughed. 'What it is to be in love,' she said. 'It's his first girlfriend.'

Martin flashed an angry glance and Roger interrupted. 'You mustn't tease. I remember my first dog and she was very special.'

Martin ruffled the Alsatian's long fur. 'What kind of dog was she?' he asked. The Alsatian barked twice and went to explore the mess she had made earlier when the coffee cups went flying.

'Oh, she was only a mongrel – bit of a mixed-up kind of dog really, but that didn't matter. She was my dog and I had her a long time. We had good times together.'

'What was her name?' Martin asked.

'Lucy. Female dogs are always the best. They don't run off like the males. Anyhow, what are you going to call this one?'

Martin looked at the keen eyes and ears. She reminded him of some work they had done at school about the North American Indians, and the fleet-footed people running silently through the forests on hunting expeditions, strong and full of stamina.

'Geronimo,' he announced. 'I'm going to call her Geronimo.'

'You can't call her that,' cried his mother. 'That's the name of an Indian chief!'

'I know,' said Martin with some pride.

'But this dog's a female,' his mother complained.

'*I* know, but Geronimo won't, will she? I bet she doesn't know anything about Red Indians.'

'It's a daft name,' scoffed Luke.

'It's a lot better than calling her Big Chief Sitting Bull,' said Martin, beginning to get angry because Geronimo was such a special, such a fitting name.

'Geronimo is fine,' said Roger. 'After all, she is Martin's dog and he can call her what he likes.'

Mrs Ashley sat down with a sigh. 'Oh well, out-voted again.'

Martin grinned up at them both. 'This is the best Christmas ever,' he said, 'and I shall always remember it.'

Mrs Ashley glanced at the broken cups and the overturned chair. 'So will I,' she said, 'and I hope I don't live to regret it.'

2 Problems

Over the next few weeks Martin made an important discovery – dogs do not arrive fully trained. They are not very good at exercising themselves either and are quite hopeless at feeding themselves. Mrs Ashley spent most of her time shouting at the dog because she was always in the wrong place at the wrong time doing the wrong thing. Roger was out at work anyway, so he didn't really know what went on during the day. Luke stumbled about the house like a zombie, a pair of earphones wrapped round his head, deaf to everything.

Meanwhile, Martin did what he could to train Geronimo. He took her out into the garden and shouted, 'Sit!' Geronimo bounced around, barking and jumping. She dashed off to the flower bed and began a furious dig, like some gigantic mad mole creating the world's longest tunnel. 'Sit!' yelled Martin.

'Get that dog off my garden,' cried Mrs Ashley, throwing open the kitchen window.

Martin tried to persuade the pup with a soft and friendly voice. When that didn't work he would try sounding really firm. But Geronimo would carry on scrabbling away at the earth, sending plants flying out between her back legs. Mrs Ashley used to throw pans of cold water over her, but Geronimo didn't mind. Not a day went past without the dog getting into trouble and Martin had a sneaking sympathy with her because of it. Hardly a day passed when he wasn't in trouble too. Martin reckoned he understood Geronimo and knew how she felt . . . not that it helped him control her. That was still impossible.

Mornings were the worst. Martin never knew what he would find when he got downstairs. There was always something.

Geronimo seemed particularly fond of books and had chewed the spine off Roger's book of Masterclass Photography. The pages were spread from one end of the front room to the other. Martin stuck the pages back between the covers and slipped the book back on the shelf, hoping Roger wouldn't notice for some time. Other books got mistaken for dog-dinners too. Sometimes Mrs Ashley found them, and then Geronimo was smacked and sent to her wicker basket beneath the kitchen table. She never stayed there long. Soon she would emerge, nose sniffing at everything, ready for another game. The catalogue of disasters grew steadily longer.

Despite this, Martin was happy. He put Geronimo on a lead and took her to the woods where he would let her go. As soon as the lead was off Geronimo was away, flying through the grass, skidding between the trees, chasing invisible squirrels and phantom rabbits. She would disappear utterly and no amount of calling, yelling or pleading would bring her back until she felt like it.

Martin didn't mind. He liked being out on his own and he would shin up a tree and sit there, watching nothing in particular and listening to the distant crashes and barks that marked Geronimo's charge through the woods. This was Martin's time of escape too, when he was free of Luke and Geronimo was free of Mum and having to keep out of trouble. There were no books to chew in the woods. There were no flowerbeds or carpets to mess up.

The only person who had some control over Geronimo was Roger. He made certain that he walked her at least once a day and although most of that time was spent on a lead because nobody could guarantee what Geronimo would do if she was off it, Geronimo was quite well-behaved. Roger tried taking her to dog-training classes, but they hadn't been very successful. Geronimo didn't seem to like being with lots of people and other dogs.

The first thing she did was try to escape back to the car. It was a manoeuvre that got the lead wrapped round Roger's legs so that his feet were suddenly whipped from under him and he fell flat on his back. It was not a very good start and certainly didn't put

Roger in a good mood. One of the exercises was supposed to help the dogs get used to meeting other dogs. All the owners went walking round and round with their pets while the dogs sniffed and wagged at each other. Sniffing and wagging was not quite enough for Geronimo. She insisted on wrestling with every dog she met and if she managed to get them to fall over completely so that she could roll on top of them, she was delighted and would leap up, barking wildly.

The lady in charge of the training class was extremely sniffy about all that and insisted on taking the lead from Roger to show him how it should be done. 'She just needs a firm hand,' the lady kept saying. It was then that Geronimo decided that rather than be taken for a walk she would much prefer to take the dear lady for a run herself, so she set off at a good gallop, dragging the yelling dog-trainer behind her. Roger and Geronimo were banned from the class and told never to come near it again.

So Roger was left to do most of the walking himself, but because Geronimo had to stay on the lead she would come back from these walks almost as energetic as when she had set off. She would charge round the house like a whirlwind, knocking things over and generally getting in everyone's way, but that, as Roger kept saying, was just her nature.

'All dogs are like that as puppies,' he explained.

Almost as if she understood, Geronimo came over, tail wagging like a windscreen wiper, and knocked Roger's coffee cup off the little table and on to the carpet.

'You got the dog,' snapped Mrs Ashley. 'You clean up the mess. Look at it – all over the carpet. It's only just been cleaned.'

Roger fetched a cloth. 'She'll grow out of it,' he said while the dog tried to snatch the cloth from his hand, thinking it was a new game.

'God forbid if that dog grows any larger,' cried Mrs Ashley. 'Look at the size of it now – three times what she was when she came.'

'Don't tell me you didn't realize the dog would grow bigger? When I first brought her home you thought she was lovely. You said she was sweet. Surely you realized she would grow? She is an Alsatian after all. How many times do you see dwarf Alsatians trotting down the street?'

Mrs Ashley got up, her knuckles white. 'You don't have to talk to me like that. I'm not stupid. I'm just saying it was a mistake to bring that creature here at all.'

'A mistake? Was it?' asked Roger. 'Was it?'

'Yes, it was!' Mrs Ashley shouted back. Geronimo, encouraged by the rising noise, let off a few barks.

'Don't you start,' said Roger, half amused.

'Oh, you two!' cried Mrs Ashley. 'You're as bad as each other. How *can* you laugh at her, after everything she's done?'

'But she's only a dog . . .'

'That doesn't matter. Look at the carpet, look at the bookcase, look at the kitchen lino that she's chewed up, look at the garden. That dog is destroying our house. Whenever the house is remotely clean and tidy, that monster comes along destroying everything she points her nose at. I can't stand it, Roger, I tell you, I can't stand it.' Mrs Ashley ran from the room and started banging dishes about in the kitchen.

Roger sat down with a sigh and eyed Geronimo, holding the dog's scruff with both hands. 'You've upset her now, you know. You're a wicked dog.' Geronimo's eyes were huge and black. Her big ears twitched. 'Are you going to behave yourself?' asked Roger. The dog sat down and gazed back at him, her face a picture of innocence. She turned her head suddenly and snapped at a passing fly. Roger groaned. 'You're just plain daft,' he murmured.

As the weeks passed Geronimo's behaviour did not get any better. Each morning brought to light new disasters. Mrs Ashley's best scissors had the handles chewed off. One of Roger's shoes was torn to pieces and spread about the floor. More and more of the carpet was reduced to tattered shreds and Geronimo started to chew the woodwork.

Martin was getting uneasy. Things were not the same in the house any longer. Mrs Ashley shouted at everybody and everything all the time. Sometimes Martin could see her almost shaking with frustrated anger. She and Roger were always quarrelling. That was how it had all started before between Mum and Dad – constant bickering, with Mum's voice getting louder and louder until the entire house had seemed to ring with the noise of raised voices. Then Dad had walked out.

Not so long ago Roger and Mum used to sit close together on the settee, watching telly. He would put an arm round her shoulders and Martin liked to see that, even though it had made Luke sneer. Nowadays they were rarely in the same room at the same time.

Martin held on to Geronimo. He would put his arms round the big dog, feeling the long, thick, warm fur. When he went to the woods he would tell Geronimo everything, talking out loud to her. It made him feel much better. Luke had overheard him once. He never let Martin forget it. He told the whole school.

'My brother talks to dogs. He's quite a loony, you know. Have you ever met anyone who talks to dogs? My brother does. I heard him just the other day, walking along the road with the dog. Do you know what he was saying? He said, "When I grow up I'm going to be a madman. I'm only half-mad now, but soon I shall be completely off my trolley!"'

Everybody looked at Martin and laughed. He could not find any words to fling back. He knew his face was bright red. He walked off to the far side of the playground, away from Luke's crowd of friends. He wanted to run, but he managed to control himself, just.

School was getting as bad as home. He felt alone wherever he was. Geronimo was his only friend. Roger had gone all moody and quiet. Mrs Ashley kept shouting about everything. Luke laughed and poked fun and walked about the house with his Walkman blaring into both ears, blissfully unaware of the problems growing around him.

Martin, however, knew that all these changes and all these problems were connected with Geronimo – one growing, energetic Alsatian pup. He wondered what would happen next.

3 Geronimo at Work

Mrs Ashley was sitting at the dining table with the local paper spread in front of her. Every so often she took the top off one of Martin's felt tips and ringed something. Luke and Martin were watching telly. Geronimo was actually asleep and Roger was watching his wife. Eventually curiosity got the better of him.

'What are you doing?' he asked. Martin switched his ears off the TV and on to his mother and Roger – eavesdropping. He already knew what his mother was doing.

'Looking for a job,' she said.

'A job? Why? We don't need the money.'

'I know we don't need the money, Roger.'

'Then you don't need to get a job.'

Mrs Ashley turned on her chair to face him. 'I want a job because I don't want to spend my life in this house with that monster around. Wherever I go she gets under my feet. She chews everything in sight. Have you seen the side of the kitchen table this morning? She's driving me potty.'

'She needs exercise,' said Roger. 'That's all. Why don't you take her out for a walk every day?'

'Because she'll never come back,' snapped Mrs Ashley. 'So, since I am being driven out of my own house by a dog, I thought I might as well do something useful that I will probably enjoy a great deal, and get a job.'

Roger appeared to be watching television, but after a while he said, 'All right, go ahead, get a job.'

'Thank you. I was going to anyway. I don't need your permission.'

'You don't have to turn everything into an argument. I wasn't giving you permission ...'

'It sounded like it.'

'All I meant was, fine, go ahead, I hope you're successful, if that's what you want.'

Roger delivered this speech from the door and Martin guessed from his whole attitude that he was fed up and was about to go off on one of his calming walks. A moment or two later the front door banged.

Mrs Ashley went back to the paper and carried on circling possible jobs.

Martin felt like lead, as if his mind had congealed inside him and turned into one heavy cold lump, now slowly sinking through his body, dragging him down with it. What would Geronimo do with no company all day? Why couldn't Mum and Roger stop arguing over every little thing? He looked at her.

'Do you have to get a job, Mum?'

Mrs Ashley's eyes glared back resentfully.

'Don't *you* start!' she snapped. She grabbed the newspaper and went to the telephone. Luke was grinning at his brother.

'What are you worried about?' he asked. 'Why shouldn't Mum get a job? We'll have more money then – might get a new bike.'

Martin stared at Luke, amazed that his brother didn't understand. 'A bike can't look after Geronimo, can it?' he pointed out. Luke started laughing.

'Geronimo doesn't need looking after. She'll be here all day long, wandering about the house. What's wrong with that?'

'But she'll be alone,' said Martin.

Luke rolled his eyes and got up. 'What's wrong with being alone?' he demanded, and went out, leaving Martin staring blankly at the telly.

Mrs Ashley got her job sooner than she expected. She had a couple of interviews and it seemed that because she was a good typist and had done some secretarial work in the past, she had the skills that quite a few employers were looking for. She started working at an estate agent's office, about five miles from home.

Despite his misgivings about Geronimo, Martin felt really proud the day his mother came home and told them about her new job. Roger went out and bought a bottle of wine to celebrate. For one short evening everybody was happy.

Now Mrs Ashley had to leave in the morning almost as early as the boys went off to school. She caught a bus and didn't get back from work until five thirty, almost an hour and a half after the boys. 'But it won't be so bad when I've bought myself a car,' she explained. 'I've already started saving.'

Even so, Martin didn't like the new routine. He dreaded opening the front door after school each day, not ever knowing what damage Geronimo may have done. With nobody at all in the house the dog went on the rampage. She was shut in the kitchen first of all. When Geronimo had finally tired of pulling things off the kitchen worktop and flinging them round the room, she had a go at the kitchen door. It was only made of thin panelling and her strong claws cut deep grooves in the wood until eventually she made a large, splintered hole. Geronimo then had the run of the house.

The hall carpet had to be thrown out. The stair banisters were chewed, one of them so badly that it snapped in Martin's hand as he examined it. The wallpaper in the front room was scrabbled at and then the dog seized the little flaps of paper and pulled at them until long slabs of chewed wallpaper hung from the walls. Everything that could be knocked over was knocked over. Anything that could be seized, worried, chased, caught or wrestled with had suffered as Geronimo got rid of all her pent-up energy.

Whenever Martin came home Geronimo rushed eagerly to him, leaping up and trying to lick his ears off in her usual enthusiastic way. She was a picture of innocence and, of course, she *was* innocent. How was she to know that it was wrong to kill cushions?

Soon there was another major row. Mrs Ashley accused Roger of bringing home a monster, a Frankenstein, a Baskerville hound. Roger accused his wife of thinking only of herself and not realizing the dog needed exercise.

'I know, I know, I know!' screamed Mrs Ashley. 'But I can't exercise her because she just runs away all the time. How can you exercise something that runs off and won't come back? You can't exercise her properly yourself, and Luke and Martin certainly can't. That dog will have to go. We can't have her in the house any longer. We can't look after her properly. I can't take any more of it. She'll have to go.'

Roger reached out and put his hand on

her shaking shoulders. 'Calm down and listen. Geronimo just needs a bit more control, that's all. We'll organize a new routine. Martin or Luke can give her a long walk before school . . .'

'On a lead,' Mrs Ashley pointed out. 'She will have to stay on a lead. That's not exercise. She needs a long run and when she runs she doesn't come back!'

'Yes, I know. But if the children take her for a long walk, on the lead, she won't be quite so energetic.'

Mrs Ashley shook her head while Martin watched, biting his fingernails nervously. 'It's no good, Roger, it won't work. You know it won't. She will have to go.'

Martin wished his mother wouldn't keep saying that. He could not bear hearing her say it over and over again. He sat down close to Geronimo and put an arm round her neck, almost as if he were afraid that she was going to be thrown out on the spot.

Roger sighed. 'All right, how about this? I'll take her into work with me.'

Mrs Ashley and Martin stared at him and he gave a nod. 'Why not?' he added.

Mrs Ashley sat down. 'I don't know why not,' she replied. 'I'd just never thought of it I suppose. But won't she rip up the workshop?'

'I'll keep her under control,' Roger assured them. 'She can stay in the car until lunch-time, then I'll take her out to the park and give her a good run.'

'But that's a great idea!' cried Martin, relief sweeping over him like a huge wave. Mrs Ashley looked at her son's happy face and then at Roger, while Martin gave Geronimo a mad cuddle.

'Give it a try then,' sighed Mrs Ashley, not at all convinced.

The new plan was put into operation the next day. Geronimo was very eager to explore the delights of Roger's car and they all laughed when the huge Alsatian sat gravely on the front passenger seat and stared out through the windscreen with her long tongue hanging out. Roger gave a cheerful wave and drove off.

Mrs Ashley was in a really good mood at breakfast. Just like old times, thought Martin. Even Luke seemed to be affected and on the

way to school he didn't tease or push or
shove. Things went well at school too. Much
to Mrs Thorpe's surprise, Martin finished the
work he was given.

It was strange going home to a quiet tidy
house. There was nothing to clear up. There
was no dog jumping and barking the moment
the key turned in the door. Mrs Ashley had
left a snack on the kitchen table for the boys
to eat when they came in. Martin sat in front
of the telly and waited for Roger's return.

Mrs Ashley came in and collapsed on the
settee saying what a busy day she'd had.
Martin made her a cup of tea. When he took
it to her she grinned and pointed at her shoes
which she had kicked off. 'If that dog had
been here she would have swallowed those by
now! Isn't it deliciously peaceful? Just feel it!'

Half an hour later Roger's car scrunched
on to the drive and Geronimo came flying in,
barking furiously in a series of dog greetings.
Mrs Ashley hastily gathered up her shoes and
slipped them back on. Roger came in slowly
from the car.

'How did it go?' Mrs Ashley asked,
pushing Geronimo to one side. Roger

regarded them silently. He beckoned with one finger and they followed him outside. He opened the car's rear door and they peered in. Most of the padding that had covered the inside of the roof was hanging in long torn strips. The back seat was ripped, and grey stuffing spilled out of the gash where Geronimo had stuck her nose in and worried it.

Mrs Ashley was quite calm for once. Perhaps because it wasn't her car. She looked calmly at her husband and said, 'Do you think the dog has rabies?'

'It's not funny,' snapped Roger.

'Did you take her into work?' asked Martin anxiously.

'Yes, I did. That wasn't exactly a roaring success either.'

'What happened?'

'It's difficult to know where to start. She put her muddy feet all over my boss's white shirt and new suit. She chewed up one of Tina's shoes – she's the secretary and she takes her shoes off under the desk while she works. I had to give her twenty pounds for a new pair.'

'Twenty pounds!' cried Luke, surfacing from his Walkman.

Roger nodded and went on. 'When I went down to the workshop that dog almost got herself sawn in half. We're making some new benches and there was some best quality beechwood on the saw being cut into lengths. Geronimo thought it was a stick I suppose. Anyway, she sank her teeth into it and tried to pull it off the machine. I got to her just in time and yanked her away before the saw sliced her nose off. The wood had to be thrown away because there were teeth marks all over it.'

For a while they stood in silence, with Geronimo sniffing round their legs, blissfully unaware of her crimes and all the problems she was creating. They stared into the damaged car.

At last Mrs Ashley spoke. 'She does have to go,' she said firmly. 'There's no doubt.'

4 More Crimes

It had been such a good day until then. Now all the brightness vanished as if great clouds had swirled up out of nowhere and blotted out everything.

'You can't!' Martin shouted. 'You can't get rid of Geronimo. She was my Christmas present. You gave her to me.'

'Cry-baby,' muttered Luke and he walked back into the house.

Mrs Ashley went to Martin. 'I'm sorry,' she began. 'Surely you can see how it is? She's ruining everything.'

'She's not, she's not. You are ruining everything,' shouted Martin, getting out of control. Mrs Ashley's patience disappeared.

'Oh, this is stupid,' she said angrily. 'I wish that dog had never come near us. I wish she'd never been born.' Mrs Ashley walked up and down the drive, forcing her fingers between each other and pressing her teeth together so that the muscles round her jaw twitched on both sides.

Roger watched her. 'Maybe it's the best thing, eh?' he said to Martin. 'We'll find a good home for her.'

'No!' said Martin.

'We'll find her a good home with a really nice family who can exercise her and look after her. We're not looking after her properly, Martin. We could get another dog – maybe a bit smaller – one that doesn't need so much exercise.'

'No!'

Mrs Ashley started. 'She's destroying the house, Martin. She's destroying the car. She's even tried to ruin Roger's furniture factory. We'll get a poodle or something.'

'No!' A poodle! It was like replacing a Porsche turbo with a bicycle. Why couldn't they understand that he didn't want another dog. He wanted Geronimo.

Mrs Ashley went to the front door. 'I'm going to ring the local newspaper now and put an advert in,' she said, and disappeared inside. Roger stood with Martin for a moment, then patted him on the shoulder and went in without saying anything further.

Martin leaned back against the car. Geronimo started a new hole in the garden, plunging her nose beneath a rose bush. 'I'm going to keep you,' whispered Martin, as much to himself as the dog. 'I am.'

When he went indoors his mother was just putting the telephone down. She looked at him with a determined expression.

'The ad's in the paper. It comes out at the end of this week.' She turned on her heels and went to the kitchen, where she started banging about noisily with saucepans and plates, preparing supper.

Roger stood in the doorway, watching Martin. 'I'm sorry,' he said. 'It's all for the best.'

Martin looked at his stepfather, hoping that Roger could feel all the things that he was feeling. Inside his head his brain kept saying: not even you, not even you would stick up for Geronimo. You all want to get rid of her. None of you love her.

Martin pushed past Roger and stamped upstairs. He lay on his bed and started to think. There must be something that he could do to prevent the coming disaster, but what? By the time he fell asleep that night he still hadn't got an answer.

Martin was quiet at breakfast next morning. He was silent going to school. He didn't do any work. He was still wrapping his brain round the problem of what to do. In the playground Luke spread the word that Martin's dog was going because she was so badly behaved.

'Must be a pretty stupid dog,' said Terry.

'She's not,' Martin insisted.

'Keep your hair on. Don't get your knickers in a twist,' said Terry. Martin swung his fist and caught Terry on the ear. Terry clapped both hands to the side of his face and yelled. Martin stuck his fists in his pockets and walked away, but Terry's friends were already running after him, pushing and shoving. 'Hey – what did you do that for?'

'Oh, go away,' muttered Martin, trying to break away from them.

'Don't you barge me,' shouted Carl, shoving Martin with both hands so that he banged against Tony. Before he knew it, he was in the middle of a brawl, with Carl and Tony and Steven all on to him. He lashed out with his hands and feet as they threw themselves on his back and tried to drag him down. One of them cried out as Martin caught him with his foot, but his own breath was knocked clean away with a staggering belly punch. Somebody hit his head and he fell forward.

A whistle blew and voices shouted. The blows stopped. Martin got slowly to his feet. Mrs Thorpe came marching over to the little group. 'What's been going on?' she demanded.

'Martin hit Terry in the face.'

'I didn't!'

'You did. You hit him on the ear.'

'That's not in the face, is it?'

'And you kicked me on the leg,' claimed Tony.

'He split my lip,' said Carl. Martin stood silent, but listening.

The list of crimes grew, just like
Geronimo's. When they had finished all he
could say was that he hadn't or he didn't.

'Anyway,' he went on. 'They started it.'

There was a loud outbreak of amazement
and the crimes were listed all over again. 'He
hit Terry!'

Mrs Thorpe cut in. 'That's enough, boys.
You know perfectly well what the rules are
and fighting is not, is NOT allowed. Go and
stand by that door until playtime has
finished. You've missed the rest because of
your foolish behaviour. I'm surprised at you,
Martin. I hope you realize the shame you've
brought on yourself.' The boys trooped
away, still muttering dark threats.

That afternoon Steven managed to pinch
Martin's pen while he was fetching a book.
He unscrewed the barrel and squeezed the
cartridge so that ink flooded Martin's piece
of writing. Then he screwed the barrel back
in place and bent his head over his own
work.

When Martin returned he found his pen
lying on his book in a pool of ink. If Steven
hadn't stopped work to look up and grin at

him, Martin might just have thought his
pen was leaking and it was all an unfortunate
accident. There was nothing accidental
about the sniggering grin on Steven's face.
Martin ignored it and fetched a clean piece
of paper and started his work once more. He
waited and watched.

It was not long before he got a chance for
revenge. Steven got up to get something and
when he returned Martin stretched one leg
beneath the table and pushed Steven's chair
back just as he sat down. Steven crashed
backwards with a startled yell.

'What is going on?' demanded Mrs Thorpe.

'Steven fell off his chair,' explained Tracy.

'I didn't!' said Steven, struggling up, his
red face appearing over the table top.
'Somebody pulled my chair away.'

'It was Martin,' said Terry. 'I saw him.'

Mrs Thorpe looked sternly at Martin.
'Come here,' she ordered. Martin got up and
walked to her desk. He could feel the whole
class watching, thirty-three pairs of eyes
burning into his back as he stood there, hot-
faced and embarrassed. 'That is an
extraordinarily stupid and dangerous thing

to do. You know very well that one must never, ever pull chairs from under people as they are sitting down. I want to speak to you at the end of school. Don't forget.'

Martin went back to his seat, not daring to look at all the eyes he knew were still on him. Just as he reached his chair it wasn't there and he fell through nothing and crashed to the floor. The ground hit him with a jarring thud and he banged his head on the back of his chair. Somebody had pulled it away.

The whole class began to laugh. Mrs Thorpe raised her voice, but some of them just couldn't stop. He could see their laughing faces, watching him and grinning. He couldn't stand it. He got up and walked into the cloakroom. He took his jacket from the peg and shoved his arms into the sleeves. Then he walked out of the cloakroom door into the bright air and started for home.

He felt, rather than saw, all the faces at the window. He knew he mustn't turn and look back. He kept on walking and waiting, waiting for someone to stop him. He seemed to be walking forever. He reached the school gates and passed between them. Now he was walking on the pavement by the main road, heading for home. Nobody cared. They didn't even want to stop him walking out of school. They didn't care about him at school and they didn't care about him at home.

'Martin! Stop!' Mrs Thorpe's voice was raised above the noise of passing traffic. He went on. She put a hand on his shoulder. 'Martin, what are you doing? Whatever is the matter?' He stopped, facing away from his teacher, not wanting to look into her face. 'Come on. Let's go back.' He pulled his shoulder away from her hand. 'Come on,' she said gently. 'Let's go back. You can't walk home from here. It's much too far.' She put a hand back on one shoulder and turned him round.

They began walking back to school and as they walked Mrs Thorpe talked. 'What would you have done? What do you think your parents would say if they knew you'd walked out of school? I know the class laughed at you, but they didn't mean any harm. They're very sorry about it and were extremely worried when they saw you walk out like that.'

'They don't care,' muttered Martin.

'Of course they care. We all care.'

Martin did not believe her. She didn't even know what it was all about. How could she care? He allowed himself to be led back to the cloakroom, where he hung up his jacket. He went into the classroom without looking at anyone, sat down in his seat and started writing. Nobody spoke to him and soon they were all getting on with their work.

At the end of the afternoon Mrs Thorpe spoke to him again. 'I shan't tell your parents this time,' she said. 'I know you were upset by the fight in the playground and then when you fell off your chair, but running away from school is not the answer. You can't solve anything by running away. You have to face up to it.'

His teacher looked steadily at his face. Martin gazed back at her, his mind elsewhere. She didn't know. She just did not know about anything, he said to himself. He allowed her to finish, collected his coat and went home. A new idea was beginning to take shape in his head.

5 Martin Is Ill?

As soon as Mrs Ashley got home from work, Luke started crowing. 'Martin got in a fight today. He got told off by Mrs Thorpe.' Then he shoved his Walkman back over his ears. Mrs Ashley put her bags on a chair and took her coat off.

'Is it true?' she asked, going to the kitchen to put the kettle on.

'Yes.'

'Why?'

'What do you mean?' asked Martin.

'Why were you fighting?' Martin stared at his mother through the kitchen doorway, wondering why she didn't ask if he'd been hurt.

'Oh, it was nothing,' he murmured.

'Doesn't sound like nothing if Mrs Thorpe told you off.'

'She told everybody off,' said Martin.

'Well, what did she say to you?'

'She told me not to fight,' cried Martin, as if it wasn't obvious.

'No need to shout,' said his mother sharply, but she said nothing more and Martin wandered back to the telly. His mind wasn't on the programme at all. He was slowly fitting plans together. Everything was beginning to take shape at last. He waited until his mother came through with her cup of tea and settled down with her feet resting on the coffee table. Luke was watching telly and somehow listening to his Walkman at the same time. Martin went quietly upstairs.

At the top he stopped and listened carefully, then tiptoed into his mother's bedroom, going straight to the big double wardrobe. It had a full-length mirror down one door, and as he approached Martin could see himself, tiptoeing towards himself, his face strained and anxious. Again he stopped and listened in case anyone should

114

be coming up. He opened the door. The catch clicked and made him wince. Martin peered inside, pushing the dresses to either side and holding them back. There it was, lying in the blue canvas bag on the floor, just where he remembered it being when his mother last put it away.

He bent down and lifted the bag out, shoved the dresses back and pushed the door shut. With a bit of luck nobody would notice it was missing. Martin hurried out. There was still no sound from downstairs and he went straight to his bedroom and shoved the bag under his bed. Then he sat down to think, and to let his thumping heart slow down.

That was the first stage – he had got the little tent. Somehow he would have to get it outside and hidden in a place where he could pick it up later. Maybe he could take Geronimo for an early morning walk and do it then? There was a burst of noise from downstairs. Roger and Geronimo had returned.

Martin hurried down and the Alsatian came pounding up the stairs to meet him halfway, so they ended up in a heap on the stairs.

'At least somebody is pleased to see her,' said Roger.

'How did it go?' asked Mrs Ashley from the doorway.

'I thought I'd keep her in the office on a lead. I couldn't leave her in the car again, not after what she did yesterday.'

Geronimo disentangled herself from Martin and went flying across to Mrs Ashley. 'Get down, you stupid brute. Oh look! That's another pair of tights ruined. Go on, get away!' Mrs Ashley pushed her to one side and the dog went thundering into the front room to launch a new welcoming attack on Luke.

'Well, what happened at work?' Mrs Ashley asked her husband.

'I took her in on the lead and tied it round the leg of my desk. The first thing she did was pull the entire desk over.'

'No!'

'She did – just like that. That dog is amazingly strong. I would never have believed it. I was sitting there and all at once

116

the desk jerked from beneath me and it was on its side. Everything fell off of course, all my drawings and plans, my cup of coffee, pens, stapler, typewriter, everything – all over the floor. Then she went mad, dashing round and round in the wreckage.'

Roger was leaning back against the stair rails, arms folded, watching Geronimo in the front room battling with Luke.

'What did everybody say?' asked Mrs Ashley.

'Oh, Tina laughed. She was in fits. I thought she'd never stop. The more loudly she laughed the more Geronimo barked. Anyhow, that wasn't all. I cleared everything up. I shall have to redraw half those plans because they've got coffee stains on them. At lunchtime I took her over to the park. That was OK until she found some poor woman and her two kids having a picnic.'

'What did she do?'

'Stole their sandwiches. She scoffed the whole lot while they ran for safety. I think they thought their last hour had come and that she was going to start eating them next.'

'Is that all?' asked Mrs Ashley wearily.

'Not quite. In the afternoon I tied her lead round the water pipes. I didn't think she would be strong enough to rip *those* from the wall, and she wasn't. She chewed up her lead instead.'

Roger pulled a short length of frayed leather from his pocket. 'She dashed down into the workshop. Lucky we didn't have anything on the machines this time and she didn't cause any further damage. I caught her in the end, but it was the sheer hassle of it all – having to chase her from one end of the building to the other. It's ridiculous.' Roger gave a long sigh.

Mrs Ashley nodded slowly. 'Never mind. That advert should be out tomorrow.'

'It can't go on,' said Roger. 'I can't take her into work again. My boss has banned her.'

Geronimo came panting from the room and wandered round their legs. 'You hear that?' said Mrs Ashley to the dog. 'You've been banned. You're a disgrace.' She looked up at Martin, still sitting on the stairs. 'What have you got to say about it, eh? She's your dog.'

That's brilliant, thought Martin. When she gets into trouble she's my dog, but when they want to get rid of her I'm not allowed to say anything. 'She's all right,' he said rather lamely.

To Martin's surprise Mrs Ashley started to smile. She put a hand to her mouth and her face crinkled up. She began to splutter and suddenly she was laughing and laughing. Roger looked at her and started laughing too. He tried to bite it back, but it all burst out like a volcano erupting. He kept pointing at the Alsatian and trying to say, 'She's all right! She's all right, that dog!'

'She only pulls desks over!' yelled Mrs Ashley, tears running down her cheeks.

'And eats armchairs!' spluttered Roger.

'And people's picnics!'

Martin ran upstairs, threw himself into his

bedroom and slammed the door. Even so, he could still hear their hysterics. He flung himself on to the bed and pulled a pillow over his head. It wasn't fair. It wasn't right. Well, it wouldn't be long before he and Geronimo showed them all. He only needed a bit of food and some money now, and the opportunity to slip away. Somehow he would have to give Luke the slip on the way to school. No, that was impossible. If only he could stay at home by himself. Suppose he was ill? Would Mum stay at home to look after him, or go off to work? It was worth a try. If it didn't work, he would have to think of something else.

Martin set his alarm watch for early morning, when he knew nobody else would be up. As it turned out he was awake long before it went off. His nerves had kept him awake most of the night, running over plans and all the different things that might occur.

At six o'clock he crept downstairs and made himself a hot water bottle. It was the middle of May and he certainly wasn't cold, but the bottle was central to his plan. He went back to bed and waited. An hour later

Roger and Luke got up. Then Mrs Ashley stirred. Roger took her a cup of tea.

'You awake?' Roger called through Martin's door. Martin didn't answer and the door opened. 'Wakey, wakey,' said Roger, smiling.

'I don't feel well,' Martin mumbled.

'Oh. What's the matter?'

'My throat hurts and my head aches.'

'I'll order your coffin,' said Roger cheerfully, but Martin didn't smile back. 'Are you serious?' Roger asked. 'I'll get the thermometer and we'll take your temperature.'

Martin listened to the disappearing steps and pulled out the hot water bottle. He held it to his forehead and let it stay there until he heard Roger returning. He came in and sat on the edge of the bed. Roger put a hand to Martin's head. 'Hmm. You do feel a bit hot. Let's see what the wonders of modern science can tell us. Stick this under your tongue. I'll be back in a couple of minutes.'

Roger left Martin with the thermometer firmly in his mouth. Martin could hear him talking to Mrs Ashley in a low voice. With thumping heart Martin pulled out the bottle and held the thermometer against it. He knew he mustn't do it for too long, remembering how Luke had once stirred a cup of tea with a thermometer and the tube had exploded because of the heat. He counted to ten, then pushed the bottle to the bottom of the bed with his feet.

Mrs Ashley came in and bent over him. 'You all right?' she asked. Martin shook his head. She took the thermometer out and held it up to the light. 'You've got a temperature,' she announced. Martin's heart leaped. 'Now what can we do? I've got to go to work today. So has Roger.'

'I'll be all right,' said Martin. 'I only want to go to sleep.'

Luke poked his head round the door. He rolled his eyes. 'He's shamming. He just wants a day off school, poor little thing.'

'Leave him alone,' said their mother. 'Time you were on your way to school anyway.' Luke shrugged his shoulders and went downstairs. 'Well, if you're sure you'll be OK. Maybe Roger can take Geronimo into work just once more.' For a second Martin panicked.

'No. Leave her behind. She can look after me.' He smiled.

His mother sighed. 'OK, if that's what you want. I'll leave some lunch for you on the table.'

'I don't want any,' said Martin weakly.

'Luke can tell Mrs Thorpe you won't be in today. I'll get back as soon as possible. Are you quite certain that you'll be all right? I'll leave Mrs Jenkins' phone number in case you need anything quickly.' Martin nodded and turned to the wall.

Not much later he heard the door open and shut several times. His mother called from the bottom of the stairs, 'I'm off now. The others have already gone. Hope you get well soon. Bye.' Then there was silence. Martin and Geronimo were alone.

6 The Great Escape

Wait, said Martin to himself. Keep calm and don't rush. One of them might come back for something. He lay listening to the silence – at least, the almost-silence, for Geronimo was doing something noisy downstairs in the front room. Martin got quietly out of bed, went to the window and looked out. He stood at the door and listened. Then he hastily dressed and pulled the tent-bag from under the bed. He rummaged through his drawers and found an extra jumper.

Hurrying into Luke's room, he searched high and low for his brother's big army penknife. He found the Walkman and considered whether to take that. Eventually he decided against it and continued to hunt for the knife. He found it five frustrating minutes later, stuck in the dartboard in the treble twenty.

Downstairs Geronimo went mad when she saw Martin. She growled and ran rings round him while he laughed at her. 'Geronimo – we're going and nobody can stop us! We'll be together and they won't take you away.'

Martin went through to the kitchen and found an old carrier bag which he loaded with his kit: the lunch his mother had left him, the blue sleeping bag from the airing cupboard, Roger's torch and a large box of matches. He searched the kitchen cupboard and found a couple of soup packets and a tin of frankfurters. He stuffed his jacket on top of everything else.

There was a five pound note under a jar on the kitchen table. Martin knew it was meant for the milkman. He stood and looked at it for ages, while Geronimo fussed against his legs. Then he thought of the days ahead and took the note and slipped it into his pocket. Last of all he got a piece of rope and

fastened it to Geronimo's collar. She pulled
at him eagerly, trying to get him to the front
door. He slung the tent bag over one
shoulder and opened the front door.

Geronimo charged out, dragging Martin
along behind. He grinned and set off at a
half-run while she strained at the rope,
practically choking herself to death. Down
the street they went, with Martin whistling.
The sun was shining. He had five pounds in
his pocket, and Geronimo. He walked until
he reached the parade of local shops where
he planned to pick up more supplies, but it
occurred to him that Mum and Roger often
shopped here. The shopkeepers would
recognize him. Martin hurried on. There
were more shops about a mile away. It was a
bit off his track, but that didn't matter.

By the time they reached the second
parade Martin was quite hot. His arms
already ached from the two heavy bags, but
he was full of confidence and marched into a
sweet shop for supplies. The shop assistant
seemed surprised at the amount he bought:
several bars of chocolate, various chews and
sweets to suck. By the time he had finished

there was little left of the five pounds. Martin wasn't worried. He had plenty to keep him going for days and days, probably weeks.

The carrier bag was now brimming over and Martin had to take his jacket out and tie it round his waist. It was too warm to wear. He retraced part of the route he'd already taken, but when he came to the footpath that led out across open country he turned down it, feeling his journey had now really begun.

For a while he kept Geronimo on the rope, but she was so much trouble, continually jerking or suddenly stopping, that he slipped the rope and let her gallop off. He was worried that she would disappear altogether, but even though she raced for miles and sometimes vanished completely, she always came back. Each time she did, Martin made a fuss over her, because he was truly glad to see her.

He picked up sticks and threw them, but she wasn't very good at fetching them and after a while Martin just concentrated on walking. He ate a couple of chocolate bars to keep his energy up. Roger had once told him that chocolate was good for energy and that was why he had bought so much. Certainly after three of four bars he felt pretty full and comfortable. Geronimo was quite fond of chocolate too. Maybe that was why she kept coming back, thought Martin.

The track was one the whole family had walked along once or twice. They had never got to the end, but had turned for home at a certain point by an old farm pond. As he passed that same pond Martin felt a surge of relief and happiness. Now he was truly away from them all, on unknown ground. From this pond they had often looked further along the path to a distant line of trees that marked the edge of a large wood. Martin had already decided that those woods should be his first stop.

Meanwhile, it was about time for lunch. He sat down on the hard earth by the path and called Geronimo. After a while she came panting out of the bushes and threw herself down beside him, in the shade, watching his every move with her bright eyes. Martin was glad she was there. He looked through the bag and decided that he couldn't face Mum's sandwiches so he gave those to Geronimo.

The woods were still miles off, so he ate some more chocolate, certain that he would need the energy. In a peculiar way it was not as satisfying as the other three bars had been. In fact, he began to feel queasy and got to his feet.

'Come on, Geronimo. We've got to keep going.' As he spoke, the tale of Captain Oates flashed through his mind: Captain Oates, ill and dying, staggering out into the Antarctic blizzard, knowing the howling wind and snow would soon finish him off. But if he didn't die, then he would slow the whole expedition down and they would probably perish too.

So, this was how Oates felt, thought Martin, his legs and feet each weighing a ton as he stumbled away from them all in his heroic self-sacrifice. The distant woods shimmered in the May heat. It was hardly a blizzard, but Martin's body felt distinctly as if it was about to collapse and die. He decided that he would never eat another bar of chocolate in his life.

After a long struggle, during which Geronimo was mostly out of sight, the woods loomed closer. The path finally disappeared into them and Martin groaned with relief as the first trees closed round him. Now he had reached the first camping ground and was hidden from view. He started to look for a suitable place to pitch the tent. It mustn't be near the path, so he struck off through the undergrowth. Twigs and leaves scrunched beneath his feet and Geronimo dashed backwards and forwards, racing everywhere in an attempt to follow a hundred different animal trails. Martin hardly noticed. He was too busy searching.

He discovered a fairly flat area where a massive beech tree had fallen, and he got the tent out. It was only a small tent, just about big enough for two. He had used it often at home to sleep in the back garden with Luke. Putting it up was not much of a problem and he felt well satisfied when it was done without any hitches. He knew what he was doing.

When he glanced at his watch it was only three o'clock. He reckoned that nobody would know yet. Nobody would be home. He sat outside the tent and wondered what

to do as it was too early for tea. He decided
to scout the woods, taking care to remember
Luke's army penknife. It was a comfort in his
pocket, hard and heavy. There were little
paths criss-crossing everywhere. Martin
marked his route with notches cut into trees.
His exploration didn't produce anything
exciting, and on the way back to the tent he
gathered some sticks ready for a fire.

Geronimo followed, watching keenly.
Every so often she tried to seize a stick from
Martin and it made him laugh. 'Geronimo –
you're an idiot!' Martin piled the sticks near
the tent. He didn't have much paper and
when he attempted to light the fire it was a
complete failure. A wisp of smoke, a quick
flame, then nothing. He used up almost the
whole box of matches before giving up and
then lost his temper and kicked the sticks
away into the wood, where Geronimo went
bounding after them.

The effects of too much chocolate had
disappeared and it was time for some proper
tea. Martin lined up his food supply.
Frankfurters? They had to be boiled and he
didn't have any water and the fire had just

been kicked into the woods. Soup? No water, no pan, no fire. That left him with chocolate, chews and boiled sweets. He didn't even have any bread. Martin began to wish he hadn't bought nearly so much chocolate, but there was nothing he could do about it now.

Geronimo had disappeared. Martin couldn't remember seeing or hearing her for some time. He stood by the tent and called. There was silence in the wood. He called again and waited, but she didn't come. Martin went back into the tent, crestfallen. He looked at his supplies again. He would have to make do with chocolate and chews. He hadn't even brought any food for Geronimo.

There was a scrunch on the leaves and the dog came trotting into view.

'Where have you been?' asked Martin with great relief. The dog looked at him blankly, her tongue hanging out. It made Martin realize that he didn't have any water for her either. How could he have forgotten so much? He wished he had brought some — and a pan, and some bread. There was too much to think about.

Martin put Geronimo on the rope and tied it round the front tent pole. She sat with her chin resting across her front paws. The sun was sinking lower and the warmth was going from the air. The trees glowed. Martin ate a few chews. They made an unusual supper and were not very satisfying, but he could not yet bring himself to eat any more chocolate.

As evening came and the sky darkened, a sense of solitude came over the woods. Martin knew he was probably the only human for miles around. He lay on his sleeping bag, looking out through the flap. There was a flicker of movement on a tree and a squirrel came down, jerking fitfully then suddenly stopping, only to start up a moment later. The squirrel gained the ground. Martin watched, entranced.

Geronimo's ears pricked up. She lifted her head, a tiny growl grumbling in her throat. Martin whispered to her, but even before he had finished saying 'Quiet now', the dog had leaped to her feet and launched herself after the fleeing squirrel. The tent pole went spinning after the dog, the rope firmly tied round it, and the rest of the tent collapsed on Martin, leaving him to struggle out. 'Geronimo! Come back, you idiot! You've got the tent pole. Geronimo! Geronimo!' A distant crashing slowly died away, leaving Martin standing alone in the darkening woods.

He looked at the fallen tent. 'Oh blast!' he muttered and set about finding a long stick that would make do as a pole. Every so often he stopped to call Geronimo, but long after he had fixed the tent there was still neither sight nor sound of the dog. Martin crawled into the tent and pulled down the flap. He struggled into the sleeping bag. Out in the darkness an owl began to hoot very close by. Martin began to wonder what he was doing there, alone and in the dark and not even Geronimo by his side. He felt hungry, stupid and miserable.

7 Something in the Night

When Luke got home from school he went
straight into the front room and switched on
the television, throwing himself down in a
chair and watching without really taking it
in. Gradually the quietness of the house crept
over him, nudging him into wondering what
was different, because there *was* something
different. What was it?

No dog. No flying Geronimo. Maybe she
had gone with Roger in the car. No Martin.
That was right, he was ill in bed upstairs.
Luke went to the kitchen, shouting 'I'm
back!' up the stairs as he passed. The lunch
that Mum had made for Martin was gone.
He couldn't be that ill. Luke reckoned that if

he'd been ill he wouldn't have been able to eat for days. He got some biscuits and sauntered back to the television. 'I'm back!' he shouted again. Maybe Martin was asleep. He plonked down and watched a cartoon.

A couple of hours later Mrs Ashley came in, putting down her bags and hanging up her coat. 'Good day at school? Have you been up to Martin? How is he?'

'I dunno. He's asleep. Anyway, he ate his lunch, so he can't be that bad, can he?'

Mrs Ashley looked down at her son.

'You wait until you're ill, then we'll see who wants sympathy.' She went upstairs. Luke could hear her calling and her footsteps going from one room to another. She came running back down. 'He's not there!' she said. 'Is he down here?'

'Who?'

'Martin, of course. Don't be stupid.'

'I'm not being stupid. Why should he be down here?'

'Because he's not upstairs!' cried Mrs Ashley, running into the kitchen and looking out into the garden. Luke got up and joined her.

'What are you doing?' he asked.

'Looking for him, of course. Are you sure he was asleep?'

'I called upstairs and he didn't answer so he must have been.'

'But you didn't go up and actually see him? You didn't bother to go up and see your brother?'

Luke reddened. 'I called up to him,' he mumbled. Mrs Ashley stood in the centre of the kitchen looking all round, her fingers fidgeting against themselves. 'Where's Geronimo?' she asked.

'Geronimo? She went with Roger, didn't she?'

'Of course he didn't take her. You heard what he said about his boss banning her from the office, or are you deaf as well as stupid?' Mrs Ashley went to the telephone and rang through to Roger. He said he was coming at once.

Twenty minutes later Roger came running in from the car. Mrs Ashley was looking wretched. 'Where do you think he is? What's happened to him?' she kept asking as Roger rushed round doing all the things she had already done, searching everywhere. 'He's not here,' Mrs Ashley kept saying while Roger searched, grim-faced. At last he came to the front room and stood looking out of the window.

'He's run away. Taken the dog with him,' said Roger. Luke felt as if Martin had punched the sense clean out of him. Incredible! Martin? His titch of a brother? Running away?

'But why?' demanded Mrs Ashley, looking at Roger with glistening eyes.

'Because he loves Geronimo, I suppose. We told him we were going to get rid of the dog, right? The ad's in this week's paper.' Roger was quiet for a moment, then he added, 'We didn't leave him much choice, did we? Either he had to stand by and see his dog taken away from him and given to somebody else, or he had to protect Geronimo himself.'

Mrs Ashley burst into tears and glared at her husband. 'You're so clever! Got it all worked out, haven't you? Well, Mr Clever-Clever, why didn't you stop him before it was too late? Why didn't you stop him?

Just because he's not your own son . . .'

Luke listened and watched, wide-eyed.
Roger was obviously stung by Mrs Ashley's
last words. He turned from her and went to
the telephone. He rang the police and then
came back, sitting down next to his wife. He
put an arm round her shoulders. 'If it had
ever occurred to me that Martin would do
something like this I wouldn't have let it
happen for the world. Martin and you and
Luke are my family. You're all I've got.'
Roger stared at the carpet. 'I'm just as scared
as you are,' he said.

'Anything could happen to him,' cried Mrs
Ashley. 'He could get picked up by
somebody in a car – that sort of thing is in
the news every week.'

'He's got a lot of sense. He'll keep out of
trouble. He can't be far away. And I don't
suppose anyone would pick him up when
he's with a large Alsatian.'

Luke was standing at the door. 'I'm going
to look for him,' he said. 'I'll find him. I'll
make sure he's safe.' Roger jumped up and
went to Luke.

'Thanks, but wait until the police get here.

I know you want to find him and we'll all
start looking soon, but let's get the police
helping too. They may want to ask you
something.'

'But all the time we stand here he could
be . . .' Luke broke off and looked at his
mother with wild eyes.

'There are the police now,' said Roger
thankfully, and went to the front door.

The police were quick and efficient,
passing on descriptions of Martin and
Geronimo to Headquarters. They also asked
many questions that made the Ashleys think
of things that hadn't occurred to them
before.

'Have you got anything he might have
taken with him, Mrs Ashley? You know,
knives or food – a sleeping bag maybe?'

Roger started. 'The tent! I'll go and look.'
He bounded up the stairs two at a time and
shouted back, 'It's not there. The tent's gone
and so has the blue sleeping bag.'

'He obviously intends to make a night of it
then,' said the sergeant, tipping his hat back
a fraction. 'Got it all worked out, hasn't he?
Bright lad, I'd say. Good thing too. At least

he's got his head screwed on right – not likely
to do anything daft – apart from running
away, that is. Right then, we'll get a search
under way, question the local shopkeepers,
that sort of thing. If you've got any relatives
or friends the young lad might have gone to,
give them a ring and check it out, will you? If
anything comes up, let us know. We'll be in
touch as soon as we have any news.'

'Can't I come with you?' asked Mrs
Ashley.

'Best not. We need somebody here. This
will be the first place he comes back to, mark
my words.'

'Oh I hope so. I hope so.'

The sergeant nodded briskly and, calling
the other policeman, they left. Luke seized
his jacket and went hurrying out, determined
to find his missing brother.

It was dark. Half a moon was shining and
throwing shadows across the trees, shafting
down between the spidering branches in an
eerie way. Martin was wide awake, even
though it was gone ten. He never thought a
wood at night-time could be so noisy. He

had expected owls, but it was the endless rustling that kept him alert and scared. It sounded as if the entire forest was wriggling and seething and scrunching and up on the march, yet he never saw a thing.

Every so often something scratched at the tent. Whatever it was kept his eyes popping and hair on end for almost an hour, until he realized it was just a branch tip brushing against the taut canvas with the movement of the wind. He broke off the tip and scrambled back into his sleeping bag, feeling relieved and stupid. His stomach was rumbling. The soup packets were still unopened. So was the tin of frankfurters. He had got so hungry earlier on that he decided he might just as well eat the frankfurters raw. That was when he discovered that he didn't have a tin-opener, not even on Luke's amazing army penknife. Instead he finished off the chocolate and chews. They weren't very satisfying.

As for Geronimo, there had been no sign of her now for almost six hours. Sometimes Martin thought the scufflings outside might be the dog returning, but he had even given up thinking that now. She had gone for good, the dog he had tried to save, the dog he had rescued so that she didn't have to go to another home. Now she'd gone of her own accord, thought Martin bitterly, and he was stuck out here in the wilderness. He couldn't go back now. He would look such a fool. Everybody would laugh at him.

Luke would probably laugh his head off. He would be taunted about it for months to come. No, he couldn't go back. They wouldn't want him back now anyway, especially after taking that five pounds. He didn't dare think what his mother and Roger would say about that. Martin clasped his knees to his chest and tried to shut out the night noises. If only Geronimo were there, with her thick fur and bright unfrightened eyes. Eventually he fell asleep.

Three hours later he woke fitfully, surfacing from a strange dream full of warnings and danger. He woke with his ears already pricked to strange, scary sounds. Out there was something snuffling and snorting, something big and heavy. It was scratching about, its body banging against one wall of the tent, a thing that breathed in raspy grunts. It was the sound of animal hunger out there, beyond the thin canvas. The whole tent shivered as the creature bumped against it, but it was so dark that Martin couldn't see a thing. His heart was leaping about like a trapped frog.

With infinite care he brought one arm out of the sleeping bag and fumbled for the torch. There was a ripping sound from beyond the flap and a tearing noise. Martin could hardly bring himself to use the torch at all. He swung round and pointed it at the noise. He held his breath, counted to three and switched on . . .

There was a badger. It was right outside his tent, with its big front paws scrabbling at the two soup packets he had left out there. The badger had torn them open and was trying to lick the last traces of powder from deep inside them. The great beast raised its head and gazed passively at the torch. It didn't seem to mind having its supper floodlit in that way and soon went back to finishing Martin's supper for him. Martin's heartbeat slowly came down to something approaching

144

normal and he propped himself on his elbows to watch this beautiful grey, black and white creature finish its supper.

The badger paused, suddenly sat down and, putting one back leg to its shoulder, had a long scratch. Martin could never describe his feelings then. He felt overwhelmed by a great sense of peace as this wild creature from the woods finished off the soup powder and sniffed about for something more. For another five minutes the badger roamed round the tent while Martin watched, entranced. Then the creature turned and shuffled away into the darkness.

Martin switched off the torch and crawled back into his bag. He wished they had all been there with him to see the badger – Luke and Roger and Mum. He shivered briefly. It was cold at half past one in the woods. He closed his eyes and slept.

8 Dogs Are Different

Every time the telephone rang Mrs Ashley jumped. Roger was sitting next to it. Sometimes it was the police ringing to say that they still had not found Martin. Other times it was any one of a dozen worried relatives and friends. This time it was the police. Mrs Ashley could tell from Roger's tone of voice that they hadn't found Martin, but she knew something had come up. She was impatient for him to finish. At length he put the telephone back on the receiver.

'What did they say?' demanded his wife at once.

'They haven't found him, but they've had reports of a large dog chasing sheep over near Tilman's Farm.'

'Tilman's Farm? Where's that?'

'Out beyond that footpath we walk on. I'm not sure exactly.'

'And the police think the dog might be Geronimo?'

Roger shrugged. 'You know what that dog's like. She's as likely run off from Martin as anything. Now she's hungry so she's after a bit of lamb chop.'

'It isn't funny,' said Mrs Ashley sharply.

'I never said it was. Seems like the farmer has phoned in to warn the police there's a dog on the loose and after his sheep. He told them that if he caught sight of it again he'd shoot it.'

Luke leaped from the settee. 'He can't do that! He can't go round shooting dogs!'

Roger shrugged again. 'Dogs can't go round chasing sheep either. They're expensive animals.'

'But do they know it's Geronimo?' asked Mrs Ashley.

'No. They're not even sure it's an Alsatian,

but from the description the farmer gave it sounds more than likely.'

'I want to go out there,' said Luke. His mother smiled at him.

'There's no point. It's ten o'clock and pitch dark. Leave it to the police. They know what they're doing.' She hunched forward in her chair, pressing her knuckles together. 'All this waiting and not knowing – it's unbearable.'

'We must be able to do *something*,' said Luke.

'You're practically asleep on your feet, Luke,' said Roger. 'You've already been out there for almost three hours, searching.'

'Didn't find him though, did I?' snapped Luke angrily.

'You did your best. I'm very grateful.'

Luke looked up sharply and searched Roger's tired eyes. 'That's OK,' he mumbled, and sank down on to the settee once more. It was true, he was worn out. He allowed his head to lean back against the cushion. He mustn't go to sleep. The phone might ring. He must know if Martin was all right. The voices in the room drifted into an endless hum, and then he was asleep.

'Ten thirty,' murmured Mrs Ashley. 'What do you think Martin's doing now?'

'He's probably put the tent up, snuck down into his sleeping bag and dreaming sweet dreams,' said Roger, trying to smile.

'I suppose that's the best we can hope for. I do hope it's true.'

Martin woke at dawn. Birds were singing everywhere and the trees whispered with tiny voices. He stuck his head through the tent flap. Grey sunlight made the wood look very different from the previous evening. There were bits of soup packet littering the ground and Martin remembered the hungry badger. It made him grin, and he struggled out of the sleeping bag. Then he recalled he didn't have any breakfast, only an unopenable tin of frankfurters. He picked the tin up and stared at it. Six frankfurters in brine, it said on the label. He could just about murder six frankfurters. He could also do with some hot toast, fried egg, bacon, beans, sausages, mushrooms . . . Martin threw the tin away.

'Geronimo!' he yelled, and the birds scattered in confusion at the unexpected noise. 'Geronimo!' He knew in his heart there was no point in calling any longer. He just thought that maybe there was a faint chance the dog would suddenly come bouncing back between the trees, charging back to him like they always did on television. Dogs never ran away on television. They were ultra-obedient and did amazing things, like rescuing babies from burning buildings and pulling unconscious drivers from wrecked cars. Martin couldn't see Geronimo doing anything like that ever. But she could eat whole carpets and ruin staircases.

Martin stuck his hands in his pockets and gazed out through the trees. She was his dog. She belonged at his side. 'Geronimo!' For a brief moment the birds scattered again, but they soon returned to the branches and filled the trees once more with their endless concert. Yet for all that noise, the woods seemed very empty and lonely. Martin felt uncomfortably close to bursting into tears. Instead he pressed his lips together hard and went round the tent, kicking the guylines from the soft earth. He packed the tent away.

He was not sure what to do next. He was

hungry and had no money left. He could hardly go to a farm and ask for food. If he went home he would probably be murdered, and how could he go back without Geronimo? Stuffing as much as he could into the carrier bag, he decided that the first thing to do was try and find his dog.

He wandered down to the path and out to the edge of the wood. In the far distance he could see a tiny flashing blue light. The police were out doing something. The car must be on one of the country lanes. Martin didn't connect it with himself at all. In the field to one side a flock of sheep were galloping across the grass. They were some distance away and Martin stopped to watch. He had never seen sheep run before and this lot were flying down the side of the hill. From this far away their huddled woollen backs looked like a sliding mass of thick porridge.

All at once he spotted something else, a big grey and brown creature loping after them down the slope. Somebody was shouting and he saw a dark figure hastily climbing over the fence at the far side of the field, waving a stick. Was that Geronimo running after the sheep? It looked like Geronimo. Martin dropped his bags and yelled. 'Geronimo! Geronimo!'

The sheep turned to escape their attacker. The man was still shouting angrily and running across the field. Martin couldn't see the dog now, only the seething crowd of sheep panting back up the hill. At that moment the man sank down on one knee. The stick was a shotgun! There was a very loud crack and the sheep split and zig-zagged away in different directions. As they broke up Martin saw a dark, still shape lying on the ground.

He ran across the field, plunging recklessly down the slope. The man had got up and was walking over to the lifeless shape, his gun bent over one arm.

'Geronimo!' cried Martin, racing downhill. The farmer stopped and waited while Martin almost fell into him.

'He was after my sheep, lad. Already killed two of them. Didn't have any choice, did I? Once a dog starts killing sheep they won't stop, not ever. Get the taste of blood, see?' He gazed down at the shaggy coat by his feet. Martin could hardly look. 'Was it your dog then? Sorry about that, lad.' The farmer stopped thoughtfully and then went on. 'You're out a bit early, aren't you? It's only just six.'

Martin bent down and touched the dog. The fur was thick and warm. There was something odd about it. Slowly he stood up. 'No,' Martin said. 'It's not my dog. I've got a dog like this one. Her name is Geronimo and I don't know where she is. She ran off, but this isn't Geronimo. My dog has two black ears and this one's only got one – look.'

The farmer wasn't too bothered. 'If you say so, lad. I'm glad it's not your dog anyhow. Not much fun having to shoot dogs. Pigeons I don't mind. Blasted nuisance they are, but dogs are different.'

There was a shout from the fence. Two policemen were standing there. One was holding the barbed wire down while the other struggled over. 'Hey! What's going on? Did I hear a shot?'

'You heard a shot, officer,' said the farmer nodding. 'That was me shooting this here sheep-killer. Killed two of my animals this morning – caught it in the act. Well, it won't be killing any more.'

The two policemen came and stood over the dog. One of them tipped back his hat and looked at Martin quizzically. 'And you'll be Martin Ashley, I suppose?'

That was it. The game was up. Martin nodded slowly. 'Where did you sleep last night?' asked the sergeant. Martin explained.

'This the lad you've been looking for then?' the farmer asked.

'Oh yes. His parents are in a right state, I can tell you.' He looked sternly at Martin.

'Are they very angry?' Martin asked, his voice hoarse.

'Angry? You must be joking! Did you really think they'd be angry? They're heartbroken, son. They're upset and worried and concerned and all the things that you obviously haven't thought of.' Martin looked up in surprise. The sergeant went on, 'Whose dog is this then?'

'It's not mine,' said Martin automatically.

'Oh I know that, son. We've got your dog down at the station.'

'Geronimo? You've got her?' Somewhere inside him a huge sun burst and lit up everything.

'Found her down at the back of the fish and chip shop late last night, didn't we? What was she doing, Mick?'

The other policeman grinned. 'Knocking over dustbins, sarge.'

Martin laughed. Yes, that was Geronimo all right, daft as ever.

'Well then, you'd better come with us and we'll run you home.'

'I've left some things by the path.'

Martin and the sergeant walked back up the field together.

'This dog of yours,' said the sergeant. 'Bit of a handful, is it?'

'Mum and Roger want to get rid of her. That's why I ran away,' Martin mumbled. 'She chews things, you see.'

The sergeant grunted. 'I had a friend with an Alsatian like that,' he said. 'It even ate the telly.'

'It didn't?'

'God's honour, it ate the telly, and half the carpet.'

'Geronimo does that,' said Martin, picking up his bag.

'Yes, they can be a right pest, dogs like that. Do you know what my pal did in the end? He gave the dog away. He had to.'

Martin was silent and wished he hadn't heard.

'He gave the dog away,' repeated the policeman. 'You'll never guess where it went though – Police Training School. If you saw that dog now you wouldn't believe it. She's a sniffer, trained to hunt out explosives, and one of the best we've got too. The training school needs dogs like that – young and wild. They make the best police dogs, you see.'

They walked back to the car without saying anything more about it. As they drove back Martin's mind was full of what his parents were going to say – and Luke too. Just to add to his feeling of approaching disaster he realized that he had left Luke's army knife in the wood. He knew he hadn't packed it. The car drew up outside the house.

9 A Good Home

They were all waiting for him. Mrs Ashley
rushed down the drive and flung her arms
round Martin. It was wonderful and
embarrassing. The policemen watched and
had a quiet word with Roger, then said
they'd be off. The sergeant got into the car.
'Come and collect Geronimo sometime,' he
said, and winked at Martin. 'Think about it,'
he added, and drove away.

'What does he want you to think about?'
asked Roger as they walked to the house.

'Oh nothing,' muttered Martin.

The next hour was filled with talking about
what had happened: how Martin had
planned it all and where he had slept.

Everything came out – all about the hot-water bottle, the five pound note, the tent, the scratching twig and the badger. Roger and Mum laughed more and more at every new thing they were told, such was their relief at having Martin back safely. Then Martin got to the shooting of the other dog.

'That was tough,' said Roger. 'It's a pity you had to see that.'

'But it wasn't Geronimo,' said Martin.

'Could have been easily,' observed Luke. 'The way she runs off all the time, she could be a sheep-killer any day.'

'Luke!' cried Mrs Ashley. 'I'm sure she wouldn't do that.'

But Martin wasn't certain of anything to do with Geronimo now. 'That policeman said Geronimo is young and wild,' he said.

Roger laughed. 'She's young and wild all right.'

'So is Martin,' said Luke with a grin, 'running off like that.'

Martin looked at the table, unable to meet Luke's eyes. 'I lost your army knife,' he confessed. 'I left it in the woods somewhere.'

Luke groaned then, surprisingly, said he
didn't mind.

'Luke spent three hours searching for you
last night,' Mrs Ashley pointed out.

Martin looked at his big brother. 'Didn't
find me though, did you? I was too well
hidden.'

'All right, cocky-bighead,' grunted Luke.

Roger looked at all three of them. 'I don't
know about you lot, but I'm ready for bed.
I'm exhausted.'

'Me too,' said Luke. And at half past eight
in the morning they all went upstairs, pulled
the curtains and went to sleep.

It was mid-afternoon before anybody
stirred. Martin was the first to get up. It was
a peculiar feeling, waking in broad daylight,
expecting it to be about seven in the
morning. He went downstairs to make
himself a sandwich. It was good to be able
to eat real food instead of chocolate and
chews. As he went to the kitchen he noticed,
almost as if he had never seen it all before,
the damage Geronimo had done to their
home.

Luke came into the kitchen and cut some

bread. 'We could go back to the wood and look for that knife,' Martin suggested. Luke nodded, his mouth full of bread. He leaned back against the table.

'What was it like up there last night?' Luke asked eventually. 'Were you scared?'

Martin wanted to shake his head and say no, of course he hadn't been scared. 'Yes,' he said, feeling like a mouse wondering if it was safe to come out of its hole or not. 'I was lonely and it was scary. I thought running away would be easy. But it was horrible.' Luke nodded slowly. Martin remembered what Mrs Thorpe had said about running away and having to face up to it in the end. At that moment in the kitchen, all the questions that had been troubling Martin came together like a finished jigsaw and he knew what he was going to do.

Later that afternoon they drove over to the police station. The sergeant was about to go off-duty, but he stopped when he saw Martin and his family walk in.

'We've come to collect the Hound of The Baskervilles,' said Roger, a cheerful grin on his face.

'That's fine,' said the sergeant, without looking at Martin. 'She's down in the pound with the other strays.' He fetched a large register from beneath the desk. 'If you wouldn't mind signing this. It says that you are the owner and you're taking her back. Just a formality. A bit more paperwork.'

Roger searched his pocket for a pen. The moment had come. Martin swallowed hard. 'I want you to keep her,' he said.

'What?' Roger wasn't sure he had heard.

'What are you going on about now?' asked Luke.

'I want Geronimo to go to the training school. Then she can be trained properly. I don't want her to be a sheep-killer and run away and get shot. I want her to . . .' He broke off and looked at his mother and the sergeant.

Mrs Ashley crouched down and looked carefully at Martin's face. He was astonished to see her eyes wet and glistening.

'Is that what you really want?' she whispered.

He nodded.

'Well,' said the sergeant, coughing loudly, 'the training school will certainly be glad to get a dog as good as Geronimo.' He slammed the register shut. 'Don't need that then, do we? There'll be some other forms to fill in – always are, aren't there? – but we can do that some other time. Now, lad, do you want to say goodbye to her?'

Roger and Mrs Ashley looked anxiously at each other, but Martin knew the answer to that too. He shook his head. 'No, I want to go home.' The sergeant nodded.

'We'll be in touch then. You're a brave lad, if you don't mind me saying so.'

Mrs Ashley gave a weak smile and they walked out to the car and drove home in silence.

Several weeks passed. Martin didn't forget about Geronimo. He had a letter from the training school to say that she had been accepted for training. He would have liked to say that, after the way she had behaved, he didn't miss her. The truth was that he did, and in a strange way the rest of the family missed Geronimo too.

Roger and Mrs Ashley busied themselves

repairing the damage the Alsatian had done. There was wallpapering, repainting and mending to do. New carpets went down in the hall and front room, paid for out of the money Mrs Ashley had been saving for her own car.

Despite this evidence of the trouble she had been, Geronimo still had a place of affection in the house. Maybe, now that she was no longer with them, it was easier to forgive her. It had not really been her fault after all. She had simply never had the exercise or the training she needed. But the evenings did seem quiet without her, and it took a long time to get used to Geronimo's absence.

One evening towards the end of July, Mrs Ashley was late getting back from the estate agent's office. Martin and Luke were getting worried about it when Roger came in.

'Mum's not in yet,' said Luke.

'Oh?' Roger didn't seem too concerned.

'She usually gets in by five thirty,' Martin pointed out. Roger put the kettle on to boil.

'I expect she'll be in shortly – probably doing some shopping.' The boys accepted that and went away.

A short while later Mum did come in. She was carrying a heavy cardboard box which she put on the kitchen table.

She put her hands in the box and lifted out what looked like an old, scruffy grey mophead. Then the mop twisted round and looked at Martin and Luke with two small, bright eyes. Mum put the dog on the floor. It pattered over to Roger and sniffed his feet. Then it trotted to Luke and sniffed him. It also had a good sniff at Martin.

'Where did it come from?'

'What is it?'

'Is it ours?'

'What's it called?'

Mrs Ashley laughed. 'One thing at a time! Well, it's sad really. The dog's name is Scrap – you can see why. She belonged to an old couple near Kemsing. The husband had a heart attack and died, and his wife is partially disabled. She's had to go into a home and she can't look after Scrap any longer. My boss is selling the house, you see, that's how I found out about it. I went to see her and told her I knew of a good home for Scrap – that I knew someone who had had to part with a dog recently and would really look after her. She was so pleased, you should have seen her face. Scrap's been trained and everything. She's used to a couple of walks a day. She's two years old and well-behaved. I thought she'd be ideal. What do you think?' Mrs Ashley looked at the others.

Martin had crouched down over Scrap and was ruffling her shaggy coat with his hands. 'Scrap,' he murmured. 'You're a beauty, aren't you?'

'Hey, Scrap,' called Luke, and the little dog turned to him.

'What kind of dog are you anyhow?'

'A bit of everything I should think,' said Roger. 'Judging by the look of her I'd say she was part spaniel, part hairbrush, part dishcloth and possibly a bit of somebody's wig.'

Martin and Luke both busied themselves stroking the poor creature until she was lying almost flat on the kitchen floor.

'Don't listen to him,' said Martin. 'You're lovely.' He straightened up. 'Who does she belong to?' he asked.

'Well, I think that this time she had better

belong to all of us,' said Mrs Ashley. 'She's everybody's responsibility. Is that fair?'

Martin and Luke nodded seriously. They all looked at Roger.

'Oh – yes – of course,' he said hastily. 'I was just thinking. Don't you think there's just a hint of shag-pile carpet in her blood too?'

Luke swung Scrap's nose round to point at Roger's ankles.

'See that man there?' he hissed. 'Kill, Scrap! Go on, kill!' Scrap sat down on the lino and put a hind leg up to her ear. She began to scratch, and as she scratched her whole shaggy coat shook and shivered like an old twist rug being shaken.

'I think she's making herself at home,' observed Mrs Ashley.

'I thought you didn't want another dog after Geronimo,' said Martin.

'I didn't think I did either. But I know you did and I know Luke did. Then when I heard about this old lady, well, it just seemed to make sense I suppose.'

'Thanks, Mum,' said Martin.

'Just one thing that old lady told me,' said

Mrs Ashley. 'Scrap doesn't like camping in tents.' She tried not to smile.

'Neither did Geronimo,' said Martin. 'And I'm not very keen on it either – unless Luke comes with me.'

Luke grinned. 'Hey, that's brilliant! Let's make a list of what we need now. We could go tomorrow!'

Roger groaned.

Fox on the Roof

1   Ghosts

Robert screwed up his eyes. He could just see
the hairy, nailed fingers scuttling along the
bottom edge of the classroom window. They
spread out black and streaked with grey, the
long tough hairs bristling against the smooth
glass. Then a single ear appeared, rising
above the window ledge like some weird
super-fast plant, slowly revolving. Beneath it
was a pair of red, tiny eyes, lying in a ragged
nest of thick black hair.

Robert held his breath, fascinated by the
slow-moving creatures that clung to the glass,
gradually taking up more and more of the
window. Their heavy bodies almost blotted
out the light now, and their long arms waved

about like bewitched branches. Somewhere in the distance was the vague murmur of voices.

'Robert? Robert!'

Somebody was laughing. A lot of people were laughing.

'Is there anybody there? Is there anybody awake inside that head?' Mr Sykes stood beside Robert's desk. He peered down at the boy's short blond hair. He bent forward and stared into Robert's right ear and he rolled his eyes.

'There's nothing in there!' exclaimed Mr Sykes and the class started laughing again. 'Broad daylight from one ear to the other!' Mr Sykes put his mouth close by Robert's right ear. 'Is there anybody in!' he cried.

Robert clapped a hand to his ear and jerked upright. He looked up at his teacher seriously. Mr Sykes gazed back. His face wore that tight smile that Robert hated.

'Well, well, well . . .' began Mr Sykes. (Three holes in the ground, Robert ticked off mentally.) 'You've decided to come back to us, have you, Robert? Which dreamland were you in this time? Was it famous fighters of World War Two, invading aliens, or the entire school going up in flames?'

Robert bent his head and the class tittered quietly. Mr Sykes went on. 'I was just pointing out to the rest of the class that it is almost time to go home, so you had better clear your desk of that extraordinary collection of junk and pick up all that mess from the floor. Right, the rest of you, you can go now.'

Mr Sykes raised his voice above the clattering of furniture and high voices. 'Make sure you leave the cloakroom clear. Now, Robert, do you think you can get home all right? You're not likely to be kidnapped by Russian secret agents on the way, or attacked by man-eating garden hedges? Try to pay attention tomorrow – it would be such a nice surprise.' Mr Sykes' mouth twisted into a tight smile once more and he walked away.

Robert got beneath his desk and picked up the few tiny scraps of paper that were lurking there like baby insects that would overnight change into huge beetles if they weren't put into the waste-paper bin quickly. He never could understand this mad insistence that the classroom should be left tidy for the cleaner every night. What was the point of having a classroom cleaner if the classroom was always left clean? There wouldn't be any work for her. She'd be out of a job. Then Christmas would come and she wouldn't be able to buy presents for her family, her children would starve to death, and she wouldn't even be able to afford to have them buried, and she'd have to keep them in old cardboard boxes until she died herself and there'd be nobody to bury her at all so ...

'Robert! Haven't you gone yet?'

'I'm just going, Mr Sykes.' He crawled out from beneath the desk and dumped the rubbish into the bin. Mr Sykes shook his head slowly.

'Why can't you be more like your sister? She doesn't seem to spend all her time dreaming.' (What does he want me to do, thought Robert – wear dresses and put my hair in a ponytail?) 'The trouble is that all this dreaming affects your work. You're falling behind the others. It's not because you can't do the work, it's because you waste so much time day-dreaming. You're just as bright as your sister, but she's miles ahead of you. It's not too late, Robert. You can still catch her up, if you make the effort.' Mr Sykes and Robert stared quietly at each other for a few moments. The tight smile was gone, but the eyes were like concrete paving stones. 'What do you think?' Mr Sykes added.

Robert nodded. Mr Sykes nodded too. Robert went slowly from the classroom and out on to the path to the house. He didn't mind if Beth was miles ahead. She could stay there for all he cared. Just because she was his twin sister didn't mean that he had to be like her. He kept trying to be somebody else. He didn't want to be Beth. He wanted to be unlike her, and since she was so good at everything that didn't leave him much choice.

He could see Beth and Mum in the kitchen as he walked past the window. The house was right next to the school – it was actually joined on to the school and shared the same roof.

Mum was the school caretaker – it was a small village school and the house went with the job. They'd only been there a year or so and Mum and Dad thought it was great. They'd been up on the council estate before, but now they had this much bigger house, even though it didn't have a garden. Dad said that didn't matter. When you had a garden, it only got fouled by dogs anyway, so why bother? In fact, there had been a long and very loud argument after that, about dogs.

Robert pushed open the door. Mum watched him as he came in. She didn't say, 'Hello!' She said, 'Coat?' Robert stopped.

'Where's your coat?' Mum repeated. 'I know it's May, but you still need your coat. I suppose you left it in the cloakroom – or is it at the bottom of the school field where you left it last week?'

'On my peg,' muttered Robert, already turning back to the school. The kitchen door banged behind him and he trudged up the path. By the time he reached the school the place was empty. Mr Sykes had left and there was no sign of the headmistress or the infants' teacher, Mrs Harvey.

The school was strangely silent. The cloakroom was half dark, even though it was a few hours to sunset. From somewhere far away came the faint ticking of a clock, the sound buried in the empty air.

Robert switched on the cloakroom light and hunted for his anorak. There were three different plimsolls on the floor and a pair of very large football boots. Robert thought the boots must be Peter's. He had feet as big as aircraft carriers. Several bags hung from the pegs, but none of them belonged to Robert.

He went to the classroom door and pushed it open. He peered round the edge. The room was huge and weird. The corners seemed to disappear into the gloom making the room appear endless. The desks stood silent and still, the chairs quite empty. It was strange. Robert didn't like to go in until he had squeezed an arm round the door and switched on the light. Even that didn't make much difference. It just made the strangeness brighter.

Robert slipped into the room and tiptoed across to his desk, wondering at the same time why he was tiptoeing, but unable to stop himself. His anorak was on the back of his chair. He should have noticed it when he put his chair on his desk, ready for his mum to come in and clean. He plucked it from the chair and turned back to the door. With his first step he heard the noise, and froze on the spot.

A long scraping sound, followed by a soft moan. Robert suddenly felt sick. His heart turned over and kicked his lunch back up his throat, making him swallow hard. Slowly he turned and looked behind him. There was nothing there. A faint murmur of voices came from beyond the classroom wall, where Mum and Beth were still in the kitchen.

Robert swung right round and back again. Nothing. He glanced quickly from side to side and headed for the door. As he reached it, the sound came again. No scraping this time but a long, soft, high moan. Before it finished, a second one began and two eerie howls drifted through the still air, one rising and one falling in a mournful duet.

Robert took a deep breath, turned and ran. He plunged out through the cloakroom door into the open, hurtled round the corner and threw himself into the kitchen, slamming the door behind him. Beth stared at her brother's white face.

'What on earth are you up to now?' demanded Mum. Robert opened his mouth and hesitated. He knew already everything that would be said, yet he couldn't just let it go without mention.

'I . . . I heard a ghost,' he started. Mum went on peeling potatoes.

'Oh, Robert!' Beth grinned at her brother. 'Honestly!'

'It's true! I heard it in the school just now. It was right in the classroom.'

Mum was silent. Beth went on grinning at her brother while he slowly turned red. 'I suppose you saw it as well,' Beth said.

'No, I didn't.'

'How do you know it was a ghost then? Anyway, ghosts don't exist, do they, Mum?' Robert looked across at Mum.

'No,' she said. 'At least, not in my school they don't. Did you get your coat? Good.' A potato peeling fell on the floor and she bent down to get it.

'I really heard it, Mum. I'm not making it up. I heard a ghost.'

'Robert!' moaned Beth.

'Why don't you shut up. It's got nothing to do with you. You didn't hear it.'

'All right, Robert, that's enough of that. Leave your sister alone. She doesn't believe in ghosts and neither do I.'

'But I heard it. I . . .'

'I've been working in that school for over a year,' interrupted Mum, 'and I have never heard or seen any ghosts. I expect it was the taps you heard. They often make strange noises.'

'Taps don't moan and scrape,' insisted Robert.

'It was taps,' laughed Beth. Mum carried on with the potatoes.

Robert went up to his bedroom. Ghost or

no ghost, it certainly wasn't taps. That was the daftest idea he'd ever heard. He wanted to talk to Dad about it, but he was doing an evening shift for the taxi firm he worked for. Robert had to go through the whole of tea and the rest of the evening carrying the memory of the howls inside his head. He didn't get to sleep until after midnight. He had listened to every tiny noise from the house and the great empty building beyond until he was too exhausted to listen to anything more at all. He didn't even hear himself snoring.

2 The Ghost Appears

'I suppose you stayed awake half the night reading. That's why you can't wake up this morning. You'd better get a move on or you'll have to go to school without your breakfast. You read too much, you do, and you don't sleep enough at night. That's why you spend your whole time day-dreaming.' Mum pulled the bedcovers away from Robert's huddled body. He brought his knees up to his chin and clasped them against his chest.

'It's half past eight,' Mum said. 'Your sister's been dressed this last hour. Even your father's up. You've got five minutes,' she warned.

Robert got dressed. If Dad was up then he could ask him about the ghost, not that there was much point. He knew what Dad would say – the same thing as Mum probably.

He clattered downstairs and helped himself to some cereal from the kitchen cupboard. Dad was sitting at the little kitchen table. He had his arms up behind his head and his legs kicked out on either side as if he were sunbathing by the sea and little waves were breaking over his bare feet.

'Dad?'

'Hmmmm?'

'Do you think there are ghosts?'

'No.'

World record for the shortest interesting conversation ever held, thought Robert. He tried again. 'Have you ever seen one?'

'No, and I wouldn't want to even if I did.'

Robert frowned. 'What do you mean?'

'I mean that even if I saw one I wouldn't want to see it. That stands to reason, doesn't it?'

Robert had a strong suspicion that there was no reason behind it at all.

'Have you ever heard a ghost?' he asked.

Dad shook his head, and at that moment Beth wandered through the kitchen. She had her coat on and her school bag. She stopped at the kitchen door.

'Robert says he heard a ghost in the school last night,' she said with a bright smile aimed at her brother.

'Oh yes?' said Dad, as Beth went out. Robert looked down into his cereal bowl. 'What did you hear then?'

'A sort of howling noise, like a moan.'

'The wind,' said Dad, and he crossed his legs beneath his chair and grasped two corners of the table with his hands.

They're big hands, thought Robert. They're like trench diggers on a JCB. He's got thick red fingers like salami sausages.

'There was a scraping noise too. That wasn't the wind.' Robert looked across at his father's face, round and pudgy, with small eyes magnified by his glasses so that they swam about.

'It was the aerial on the school roof. It was the wind moaning through the wires. There aren't such things as ghosts. Why should there be? I don't know anybody who's ever seen a ghost. That's a load of rubbish. You shouldn't believe things like that. You've got too much imagination.'

Robert picked up his bowl and took it across to the sink. He shoved it into the washing-up bowl along with all the other breakfast stuff. Then he grabbed his anorak and went to the door. His father called after him and when Robert turned to look Dad bulged his eyes and wiggled his fingers.

'Woooooooooo!' he sang, and grinned at his son. Robert shut the door behind him and went round to the school. He passed Beth in the playground.

'You didn't have to tell him,' he said.

'You were going to tell him yourself anyway.' Robert stood silent for a while, his hands in his pockets, watching the others arrive for school.

'I did hear a ghost,' he said at last. Beth looked at her brother. She was three inches taller than he was, even though he insisted he was the elder because he had been born seventeen minutes before she had.

'Ghosts don't exist,' she murmured.

'You've never seen one, that's all!'

'Neither have you,' said Beth.

'No – I heard it. Seriously, Beth, listen. You know what noises the taps and the pipes and everything makes in school. It wasn't any of those.' Beth scraped one foot on the gravel.

'What did Dad say it was?'

'Oh, he reckons it was the wind in the aerial. Do you remember yesterday evening? There wasn't any wind at all. It would have to be blowing a hurricane to make a noise through the aerial. Where's the hurricane damage? Where are the smashed cars lying on people's roofs? Where are the flying cattle stranded on chimneys? Where are the trees thrust through front windows? Where are ...'

'What are you going on about, Robert?'

'I was just pointing out the things that happen in a hurricane.'

'What hurricane?'

'The one that didn't happen last night and didn't make the aerial moan,' Robert said patiently.

'There's Nina. I'm going to play with her. I think you're going mad,' she added as she went off.

Robert found some of the boys from his class and told them about the ghost. They were interested and more or less believed him. It was great to think that the class might be haunted, even though most told themselves it wasn't really true. That way they could enjoy being scared.

The subject even cropped up in class and Mr Sykes expressed suitably grave interest.

'And who saw this ghost?' he asked.

'It was Robert,' answered Alex. 'He didn't see it. He heard it. It went wooooooooooo-ooooooooo ...'

'Thank you, Alex, that's enough to frighten the poor ghost away I should think. So, you really heard a ghost last night, Robert? Strange that we've never heard it before, but perhaps it's just arrived here recently for a holiday. Or maybe it's come to learn something.' Mr Sykes went on for some time about ghosts and in fact, the whole morning became quite interesting because they went on to write ghost stories.

As usual Robert wrote all the best and most exciting parts of his story in his head.

When Mr Sykes came round looking at their writing books, all Robert had was:

There was a ghost of Jaws and it was big and it lived in an old house where the . . .

Mr Sykes sighed. 'Stay in at playtime and finish it off then, Robert.'

When everybody else had gone out for break Mr Sykes went and sat on the edge of Robert's desk.

'I don't understand you, Robert. I know you've got a good imagination. You've often told me marvellous ideas. How come they never appear on paper? Don't you like writing stories?'

'I don't mind.'

'Are you left-handed or something?'

Robert shook his head. What difference would that make? Would he have to write his stories backwards perhaps? Did they make special left-handed paper?

'How is it that you never manage to finish a story? This happens every time. You nearly always spend your playtime in the classroom and even then you don't finish it.' Mr Sykes paused. 'Are you worried about something perhaps?' Robert shook his head.

'There's nothing at home you're worried about? Nothing at school? You can tell me, you know. Maybe I can help you.'

There's nothing wrong. Everything's wrong, thought Robert. And I don't want your help. I want my help.

'There's nothing wrong,' he murmured and began to add a few meaningless words to his story. Mr Sykes stood up and went to the staffroom for a cup of tea. When he came back at the end of play, the story was still unfinished, but now it was forgotten as they went on to other activities.

After lunch Robert looked for Beth and took her to one side. He was determined to convince her about the ghost. 'We'll both come back,' he said. 'When everybody else has gone, we'll come back and listen.'

'I don't want to,' said Beth. Robert smiled.

'You're frightened!' he cried.

'I'm not! Don't be stupid, it's just a waste of time, that's all.'

'You're scared!' cried Robert. 'You're

scared of a ghost and you don't even believe in them!'

'Shut up!' hissed Beth. 'All right, I'll come.' Robert stopped dancing round and poking his sister.

'We'll come back after school, just for a few minutes, very quietly, and listen for it,' he said. Beth nodded, and Robert grinned happily. He even managed to work that afternoon and gained some praise from Mr Sykes. Even so, it seemed a long wait to the end of the afternoon. Then it was even longer before the teachers went.

At last the school was left in silence and Robert and Beth crept into the musty cloak-room. They peered around at the shadowy coats hanging lifeless from the pegs. Robert went to the classroom door.

'Can't we listen here?' asked Beth, moving towards the outside door. She was scared, but she was determined that Robert shouldn't notice.

'We've got to go into the classroom,' insisted Robert and he pushed open the door. The top hinge gave a long squeal that made him wince and they tiptoed into the big, empty room. Robert looked at his sister's face. 'You're scared,' he said. 'So am I. My heart's thumping.'

They stared round at the huge space. There was an awful lot of emptiness for a ghost to be in.

'Do you think it's here?' whispered Beth.

'I can't hear it yet. Hello? Hello? Is anybody there?' Robert raised his voice to the ceiling. 'Hello?' There was a long silence, then the water pipes gushed and gurgled for several seconds. Beth looked at her brother and he shook his head. 'That was nothing like the noise I heard last night. You try it.'

Beth frowned, bit her lower lip for a second and then shouted.

'Hello, calling all ghosts, calling all ghosts. This is Elizabeth Duncan, are you receiving me? Calling all ghosts, are you . . .'

'Beth! You're not talking to aeroplanes!' Robert was almost in hysterics, trying not to laugh out loud in case he disturbed the ghost. Beth folded her arms sulkily. Robert tried again.

'Hello? Who are you? Where are you?'

'I'm your mother and I'm standing right

next to you. What on earth are you two doing here at this time? Stop playing daft games and get off to the house. Your tea's on the table and don't forget to wash those filthy hands and if you've left your coat on your peg again, Robert, make sure you take it with you . . .'

Mum's commands followed them out into the cloakroom and then outside. That was the end of that. It was after tea before they went out again. They went to play on the playground with their bikes, but half way round Robert almost smashed into Beth. She began to shout furiously, but he grabbed her and twisted her round and pointed up at the school roof.

Beth just had time to see a large, dark shape slip along the ridge of the roof and duck down behind the big double chimney.

It was a fox.

3 Spiderman

Beth and Robert stood in the middle of
the playground staring up at the long school
roof. Beth suddenly turned to her brother.

'That was a fox. It *was* a fox, wasn't it?'
Robert nodded. 'It wasn't a dog?'

Robert said seriously. 'It can't have been a
dog. Dogs can't climb.'

'I didn't think foxes could climb either,'
said Beth. 'How come a fox can get up there,
right on the roof?' She was still looking up
towards the double chimney as if she expected
the fox to reappear at any moment. Robert
grinned.

'They probably roped themselves together.

They must have climbed the north face using ice picks.'

'What are you talking about?' shouted Beth. 'What do you mean – ice picks and north face?'

'The foxes,' Robert explained. 'I wonder where they made their base camp? I expect they had to use oxygen masks to climb that high – must have been pretty difficult. Ow!'

Beth thumped him on the shoulder. 'Don't you ever take things seriously?' she demanded. 'That was a fox on our roof, a real, live fox. We ought to tell Mum.'

'She won't believe us,' Robert pointed out quietly.

'We'll tell Dad then.'

'Won't make any difference. Anyhow, what do you think they would do about it?'

They looked at each other. Beth sat back on her bike. 'Well,' she mumbled, 'we ought to tell somebody.' She turned the handlebars and rode back to the house.

Robert stayed for a few minutes longer. He rode around the playground, sometimes glancing up at the school roof. It gradually grew darker and the high ridge of the roof cut across the darkening sky, sharp and clear, with the big double chimney sticking up like a magician's wardrobe, right where the fox had vanished.

Robert rode slowly back to the house.

A few hours later he lay in bed, wide awake. Beth had told Mum about the fox and, of course, she had laughed and joked. What was the point? thought Robert. It was just a waste of time. Who was there to tell?

He heard Mum and Dad come upstairs and run a bath before they went to bed. His little clock said just after ten thirty. He turned over to face the bedroom wall and he stared blindly at the wallpaper. Hundreds of racing cars, all the same, were racing towards hundreds of chequered flags.

This was what puzzled him: Why should a fox go to the trouble of climbing up on the school roof? They were surrounded by open countryside. There were fields and woods and streams and hedgerows. There were rabbits and hares and shrews and voles and mice and rats and hedgehogs. He'd seen most of them himself. Why should a fox go clambering around on roof tops?

Robert suddenly jerked up. Of course he hadn't heard a ghost! It was the fox making that moaning and scraping! He lay back on his pillow, grinning madly. What an idiot he was! It was a fox all along, up on the roof, howling. He folded his arms across his chest and smiled up into the darkness of his bedroom.

Then another thought came into his head. He had heard two moans and that must mean there were two foxes. What were two foxes doing on the school roof and, come to think of it, if they were on the roof how could he possibly have heard them when he was *inside* the classroom?

There was a noise outside as Mum and Dad finished in the bathroom and went to bed. Robert yawned and listened to the small noises that came through his half open doorway. He wondered if the fox was up there now, silently padding over the cold tiles, eyes pricking the darkness.

In the morning he would go up there and see for himself. In the morning he would go up there.

*

It took ages before Mum went round to the school to get on with the weekend cleaning. Since it was a Saturday, Dad would be working until after midnight and Robert was sure not to see him until Sunday afternoon now.

As soon as Mum had gone, Robert told Beth what he was going to do.

'You can't!' she hissed. 'Mum'll go mad if she knows you're up on the roof!'

'I'm not going to tell her. It won't take long. I want you to stand guard for me. I'll get the aluminium stepladder and go on to the flat roof outside the landing window. Then I can climb over my bedroom roof and down on to the school's. It's quite safe.' He was already pulling the stepladder out from the cupboard.

'But what will I do if Mum comes back?' demanded Beth.

'Just shut the window and clear the ladder away so that she doesn't see it. Then she won't know anything about it.'

Beth followed her brother upstairs. He opened out the stepladder and climbed up to the window. He stopped for a moment when he had one foot out on the flat roof. He looked back at Beth.

'You're mad,' she whispered loudly. Robert grinned at her and stepped on to the roof.

Two sloping roofs rose on either side of him, with a thin chimney going up the side of one. That was the chimney for their front room fire. The flat area between was dirty, and large clumps of scruffy moss were plopped here and there like strange alien hedgehogs from a distant galaxy.

Robert didn't waste any time admiring the view out across roofs and gardens to the fields and woods and hills beyond. He didn't know how much time he had. He pulled himself up alongside the chimney and just managed to stretch out his fingers to the top of the roof so that he could pull himself up until he was sitting astride the roof. He knew that it was impossible to walk up the roof side. It was too steep and the tiles were fragile.

From his new position he could see the school roof a little way below. He swung his legs forward and used the momentum to work his way along the ridge of the roof until he could swing his legs down on the school side and lower himself down.

It was the only dangerous bit because the school roof had a sheer drop on the side it joined the house roof. It just sloped down to the wall and after that it was a long fall. Robert swallowed and looked away. He felt out with his feet and located the school roof and slowly slid himself down on to it.

Now it was easy. There was another flat roof between the two sections of the school roof, and that was where the big double chimney came up – which was where they had seen the fox.

Robert slid down the tiles as quietly as he could, remembering that Mum was working somewhere below. He tiptoed across the flat section, looking carefully all around. There was certainly no sign of the fox now. Robert went right round the chimney twice, but there were no tracks or anything.

He wandered up to the far end of the flat roof and looked over the edge. It was a curious sensation, to see the ground so far away. Yet it didn't seem as if it would be far to jump.

Robert turned back and then he saw the little ventilation window for the school loft. It had been covered by thin chicken wire to stop pigeons flying in and nesting. The wire was all bent and pulled back, leaving quite a large hole. Around the hole were lots of white feathers, little, white, curly feathers.

Robert bent down and put his face to the hole. He stared into the blackness beyond and caught the smell of dust and dirt and age. He couldn't see a thing. He sat back for a moment and looked at the feathers. Surely a pigeon couldn't pull that wire back? Now he was certain that the fox he had heard wasn't on the roof at all, but actually inside the school loft! So he would just have to take a look in there.

He scrambled back up the roof and worked across to the house roof. It was more difficult from this side because he had to reach up, standing on the thin edge of the school roof on tiptoe so that he could grip the house roof.

He strained upwards and moved one leg out across the slope of the house roof to get a better angle. A moment later his foot slipped and he crashed downwards, his arms flung out, trying to grip on something. There was nothing there at all. His nails scraped down across the tiles and his chin caught a great blow on the top of the roof as he came slithering down.

With arms and legs outspread he slid helplessly down the side of the school roof. He shut his eyes. He knew there was nothing to stop him. His feet slammed down into the ancient metal guttering and his legs automatically seized straight.

Robert opened his eyes. He could taste blood and his left side stung. 'I'm Robert Duncan,' he whispered to himself. 'I'm Robert Duncan.' At least he hadn't lost his memory. He looked down and saw his feet in the gutter and suddenly realized that if the guttering had been plastic and not old-fashioned iron, he'd be splattered on the playground by now.

Then he looked up at the grey roofs stretching above. He was almost in a corner where the two roofs joined. Very slowly Robert eased himself to one side so that he lay in the crook of the roofs. He flattened himself against the tiles and began to claw his way upwards, little by little, an enormous, ridiculous spider with four legs missing. Can you get spiders with wooden legs? he thought madly, halfway up the roof.

At last his fingers curled over the ridge of the roof and he hauled himself to safety. He sat astride the roof, panting and looking back the way he had come. Then he quickly slid down on to his own flat roof and clambered down the ladder.

Beth gasped. 'You're filthy and you're bleeding! Did the fox attack you?'

Robert grinned and shook his head.

'It was incredible,' he said. 'Enormous!'

'What? What was it?'

'A spider – a giant four-legged spider!' Robert felt the bruise beneath his jaw and tilted his head for Beth to see.

'Look – he hit me with one of his wooden legs!'

Beth stamped one foot angrily. 'Robert!' she moaned.

4 In the Loft

Robert leaned back against the ladder and explained everything to Beth. She wondered if pigeons could have pulled back the chicken wire. It didn't make sense that a fox should want to get inside the school loft.

'I know it's daft,' Robert agreed, 'but a pigeon couldn't rip chicken wire from a window. A dog can't get up there and it doesn't explain all the feathers either.'

'Maybe it was a cat?' murmured Beth. Robert shrugged.

'No way. It wasn't a cat we saw, was it?'

Beth was silent.

'Anyhow,' Robert went on, 'I'm going up there. You stay here and watch out for Mum.'

He pulled the stepladder away from the window and swung it round to lean against the trap door that led to the loft.

'That's no good!' cried Beth. 'That's our loft.'

'I know. It joins on to the school loft. Dad showed me when we came up here to store my old bike. The school loft is much lower than ours because the house has two floors and the school only has one. There's quite a big drop down, but there's a little wooden ladder that leads down to it. I've never been down it, but I know where it is.'

He put a foot on the ladder. Beth touched him on the arm.

'I'm coming with you,' she said.

'You can't! You've got to keep guard.'

'I don't want to and I don't have to.'

'Suppose Mum comes?'

'We'll tell her we were clearing some old toys or something. Anyhow, my torch works and yours doesn't. Your battery's run out. You told me.'

Robert grunted. 'Oh all right, but I'm going first and I'm going to hold the torch.' He stood on the steps and wouldn't move until Beth had handed over the torch.

The door to the loft was big and it was easy to climb through into the darkness. Beth crouched beside the open hatchway and glanced back at the landing and the ladder.

'Are you sure it's all right?' she asked, but Robert had already gone ahead. Beth could see the weak yellow light from the torch jumping about in the dark and she crept slowly towards it.

'Come on,' complained Robert. 'We haven't got much time. Watch where you put your feet. Make sure you only tread on the rafters and not in between.'

'Why not?'

'Because your foot will go straight through the bedroom ceiling if you do and then we really will be up the creek. Look, those are the rafters.'

'I know that!' Beth snapped. 'Where's the ladder?'

'It's over here. Be careful, the roof beams get lower here.'

The twins reached the top of the little ladder that led down to the school loft. Robert shone the torch over the drop, and then out across the long triangular corridor.

'It's enormous,' he whispered. 'Listen, you can hear Mum's vacuum cleaner in the classroom somewhere.'

A faint growl vibrated around them. Robert gave the torch to Beth and clambered down the ladder. Then he took the torch back while Beth came down. She coughed.

'It's filthy and it smells.'

'It stinks like the dustbag on the vacuum cleaner when Mum empties it,' Robert suggested.

'Urrgh!'

They crept forward across the enormous space, ducking under low, angled beams that passed from one side of the roof to the other. Robert stopped and bent down.

'Here's a trap door. Lift it up.' They both bent forward and hauled on the trap door and it lifted slowly. They put their faces to the crack of light.

'Hey! It's our classroom, Beth!'

The noise of the vacuum cleaner was much louder now. They could see the long electric flex trailing right through the classroom and into Mrs Preston's room. Robert lay on his stomach in the dust and grinned across at his sister.

'She'll never guess we're up above her. It's great. It's like spies ...'

'She might see us.'

'No. Come on, let's put the lid back down. We'd better get a move on.' He waved the torch ahead and it caught the old red brickwork of the double chimney. He straightened up slowly. 'Beth, look. That's where we saw the fox – and look! You see that little square chink of light? That's the hole which had chicken wire across it.'

They began to edge forward along the rafters. Beth clung with one hand to Robert's jumper. It wasn't at all easy to see where she was going since he kept the torch pointing forward all the time.

Just as they reached the chimney a long, low growl filled the roof chamber. Robert jumped and stepped back.

'Agh!' squeaked Beth.

'What's up?'

'You stood on my toe, you twit,' she hissed, and stared hard over Robert's shoulder. 'What is it? Can you see anything?'

The torch beam swept slowly round the dark emptiness ahead.

'Can't see anything,' muttered Robert and he stepped forward again. A soft whimpering noise came from ahead. It was a sort of snuffling wail. 'I'm going ahead to look,' said Robert.

He held the torch in his left hand and gripped the huge chimney with his right arm, working his way gingerly round the crumbly brickwork. He leaned forward and peered round the edge. A rumbling growl greeted his white face.

'Beth! Come and look! Quick!'

She stumbled towards the waving torch. At first all she could see was the shadowy bulk of Robert's back, leaning round the chimney. 'Hurry up!'

'I'm coming. Ow!'

'Now what?'

'I hit my head on a beam. Oooh!' Beth tripped over a rafter and fell against her brother. She gripped his jumper and steadied herself. Then she peered over his shoulder.

The torch light pinpointed one corner of

the loft, where the roof came sloping down and somebody, long ago, had cast away an old cupboard. One door was missing and the other was only held on by a single hinge.

Huddled inside and blinking slowly at the glare of the torch, were three fox cubs. One was lying sideways on, with his head twisted round towards the children. The other two had wedged themselves on top of the first, their chins resting on his back, and they blinked and blinked again. A tiny whimper came from one and then it turned into a wide-mouthed yawn.

'They're beautiful,' whispered Beth. Robert edged forward and one of the foxes instantly lifted its head and showed its teeth — tiny, white, sharp teeth.

'Don't go closer. You'll scare them and they might bite you.'

'They're tiny,' murmured Robert. 'We could pick them up.'

'No we couldn't. Where are their father and mother?'

'Outside, I suppose. Maybe they're hunting for food to bring back. Hey!' Robert turned to Beth quickly. 'Why don't we get them some food? We could bring it up here and feed them and then they'd get used to us and maybe we'd be able to pick them up.'

'How are we going to catch a rabbit?' Beth demanded.

'We don't need to.'

'Well, I don't see how else you expect to get food for them. You can't buy fox-food you know.'

'But there's meat in the fridge!' cried Robert.

'We can't take that!'

'Why not? It's been there for two days already and Mum still hasn't used it. It's probably gone off by now.'

'Maybe she was saving it for the cat.'

'Lucifer is as fat as a sheep already.'

Beth was silent for a moment. 'He's not *that* fat.'

'Oh come on. I'm going to get it now.'

Rather than be left behind in the dark loft, Beth followed Robert out and soon they were back in the house itself. Beth was still uneasy about the idea.

'Why don't we ask Mum first?' she suggested.

'Oh great! What do you think she'll say if she finds out there are foxes in the loft?'

They stood and looked at each other. They both knew perfectly well what Mum would say and what she would do. They'd had a wasp nest in the loft two years ago and Mum had called out the pest control people from the council. They'd killed all the wasps and cleared the nest away.

'She probably wouldn't believe us,' said Robert. 'Not even if the foxes were right under her nose.' He opened the fridge door and hunted through the shelves. 'This will do. I think it's some stewing steak. What do you think they'd like for pudding? A bit of ice cream?'

'Foxes don't eat ice cream!' yelled Beth.

'It was a joke. Come on.'

They raced back up the stairs and

clambered up the metal ladder. A loud voice yelled up the stairs.

'Beth! Robert!'

'It's Mum!' hissed Robert. 'Quick, throw the meat up in the loft so that she doesn't see.'

Beth hurled the little plastic bag up through the trap door. There was a loud splash and several drops of water rained down.

'What was that?' asked Beth anxiously. Robert bit his lip.

'I think you've just thrown the stewing steak into the water tank!' he said.

5 Water, Water Everywhere

Mum came up the stairs. As her face reached the level of the landing she slowed down.

'I see. No wonder everything was so quiet round here. What do you think you're up to?'

Robert glanced at Beth. She hesitated, then mumbled, 'I was going to put some of my old toys up in the loft. That's all.'

'Oh yes? And I suppose Robert's helping?' Robert nodded. Mum looked from one to the other several times. She sniffed. 'Have you cleared your bedroom yet, Robert?'

'I'm halfway through.'

'You're always halfway, but you never finish.'

'I can't help it, Mum. The tidy bit gets untidy when I tidy the other untidy bit, so there's always a tidy bit and an untidy bit and you always look at the untidy bit first.'

'Robert,' Mum said coldly, 'you are talking nonsense. Go and clear your room. If you're serious about putting old toys up there, Beth, then make sure you put them by the trap door. Don't go inside, it's dangerous.'

Beth stole a glance at her brother. He was smiling. Mum clumped back down the stairs.

They listened to the kitchen door shut and her footsteps pass round the side of the house and back to the school. Then they both made a rush for the ladder at the same time, and scrambled hastily into the loft.

Robert bent over the water storage tank and peered in.

'I can't see the meat, but it can't have landed anywhere else. Shine the torch across the bottom. It must have sunk – look! There it is. Blimey, Beth, it's right at the very bottom. I can't reach it down there.'

'Don't say blimey, it's rude.'

'It's not – well, not very.'

'You still shouldn't say it.'

214

'Why not? Dad says words like ...'

'Don't!' hissed Beth. 'Look, just get the meat.'

'I can't. You can see how much water is in there. I suppose I could put my scuba-diving gear on and my aqualung and everything. Or you could lend me your rubber ring ...'

'It's not funny,' snapped Beth.

A weird moan drifted up from the school loft. She grasped Robert's arm. 'They're hungry. We must get that meat to them.'

'Oh all right. Listen, we'll have to get rid of some water. If we turn on all the taps then the water will go down in the tank and I can get the meat before it refills. You go down and turn all the taps on.'

Beth thought for a minute, but she couldn't think of any better idea so she hurried down the ladder and rushed to the bathroom. She turned on the bath taps and the basin taps and pulled the toilet chain. Then she dashed downstairs and turned on the taps in the kitchen. Panting, she stumbled back to the landing and struggled up into the loft.

'Is it working?' she gasped. Most of Robert

had disappeared over the side of the water tank. His legs were waving in the air and when he spoke his voice echoed round the metal tank so that he sounded like a strange monster from the deep.

'Got it!' he cried, and jerked himself back to his feet.

'That water was really cold.' He held up the packet of meat triumphantly. 'Come on!'

They staggered from rafter to rafter, with the torch beam bouncing about in the dark. At last the double chimney rose up in front of them.

'Be careful,' whispered Beth. 'The parents may have come back.'

Robert glanced round the chimney. 'It's all right. They're not back yet. It's a good thing we thought of this meat or the cubs might starve. It might take ages for their parents to find them food.'

The three fox cubs sat up straight and stared back at the children. Their lips curled back and they began to snarl as menacingly as they could. The biggest one struggled to his feet and all his hair prickled up. He gave tiny jumps and spat furiously at the

approaching children. Beth put a hand over
her mouth and giggled.

'Doesn't he look angry? Here, we've
brought you some food. Don't talk to us in
that tone of voice, you cheeky monkeys.'

She laughed.

'They're not cheeky monkeys. They're
cheeky foxes. Come on, you lot, we just want
to put some meat down for you.' The big cub
leaped forward and landed on all four paws,
snapping and spitting with fear.

'Isn't he sweet!' Beth exclaimed.

'You won't think he's sweet if he sinks
those teeth into your leg. We can't get any
closer. Open the bag and we'll throw the
meat from here.'

Beth tore open the plastic bag and they
each took handfuls of steak and threw it
towards the fox cubs. They weren't very
good shots. Some meat landed behind the
cubs, some in front, and two or three strips
fell across their backs and heads, or bounced
off their noses.

The cubs watched each little piece of flying
meat and snapped at it in passing so that
more than once they bit each other instead.

By the time the meat had gone, Robert and Beth were clutching the chimney in hysterics.

At last the fox cubs settled back in the bottom of the old cupboard. They looked very content and were quite happy to just keep one eye open on the children while they had a little doze.

'They're fantastic,' Beth said softly.

'I told you there were foxes up here,' Robert reminded her.

They stood quietly watching the three furry bundles. Gradually noises from beyond the loft filtered through into their brains. There was a far-off, constant gushing sound, like a distant waterfall thundering in the dark jungle.

'What's that hissing sound?' Beth asked eventually.

'Oh blimey! It's the water! You left all the taps running, Beth! Quick!'

They dashed back across the rafters, bruising their heads and arms and shins on the low rafters which they didn't have time to see in their haste. Robert squirmed up the short ladder and back into their own loft.

Water was pouring into the storage tank

and just as fast going out again to all the taps in the house. Robert glanced into the tank and then almost fell down the ladder and on to the landing.

'Come on, Beth!'

Beth came down more slowly. Her hair was covered in dust and cobwebs and there were long streaks of dirt smudged all over her clothes. She plunged down the stairs and even as she did so a dismayed yell came from the bathroom.

Beth switched off the kitchen taps. That was all right – the water had gone straight down the plughole. She checked everything and then tore back up the stairs and dashed to the bathroom. She stepped straight into a large flood, and just as quickly jumped back on to dry land.

Robert was standing in the middle of the flood and trying to mop it all up with a face flannel. He wasn't having much success.

'What happened?' cried Beth.

'It was this stupid flannel. Somebody left it in the bath and it blocked up the plughole. Don't just stand there, do something.'

Beth seized a big bath towel and threw it

across the floor. They watched it quickly
darken as the water soaked into it. Then they
picked it up, wrung it out over the bath and
threw it down again. Gradually the flood
became a lake and the lake became a puddle
and the puddle became a slightly wet floor.
They wrung out the towel for the last time
and stood there holding it and looking at it.

'What do we do with this?' asked Robert.
Beth shrugged.

'Come on, Beth, you should know. You're
a girl.'

'What difference does that make? You use
towels just as much as I do. I know! Put it in
the airing cupboard in my bedroom. It will
probably dry out before Mum even realizes
that there's anything wrong.'

She took the towel to her room and shoved
it into the cupboard where the hot water
tank stood. Mum always used it for airing the
clothes after they'd been through the
washing-machine. Beth had hardly shut the
door before there was a shout from
downstairs.

'Robert! Beth! Come down here!'

They looked at each other. Mum didn't

sound too cheerful. Maybe she'd discovered the loss of the stewing steak? They went down slowly to the kitchen, but Mum wasn't in there.

'I'm in the front room,' she called.

They stood in the doorway. Mum was standing in the centre of the room with one hand held out flat, palm upwards. As they watched, a drip of water splashed on to her skin. Then another. Then another. Mum frowned.

'What's been going on? Why is there water coming through the ceiling? And good grief! Look at you both! What have you been doing? Just what's been going on?'

Robert swallowed hard and shuffled his feet. He screwed up his eyes and stared at the ceiling, where a large damp patch had formed, just to one side of the light flex. There was a small sob from by his side. Beth sniffed and wiped one eye.

'It was the cubs,' she began. Robert suddenly woke up.

'It was the Cubs,' he almost shouted. 'You see, the Cub Scouts are supposed to do good deeds for people and I thought I'd clean the bathroom floor for you, Mum, but I spilt my bucket of water by mistake. It was a mistake, Mum, it was a mistake. I mopped it up as quick as I could, and Beth helped.'

Mum looked angry, astonished and surprised, all at once. She glanced up at the ceiling. Another drop fell to the carpet.

'I . . . I don't . . . it doesn't make sense. Is there any more up there? For goodness sake, Robert, you're not even a Cub!'

'But Beth's a Brownie,' Robert pointed out.

Mum stepped back and sat down heavily on the settee. She smoothed her hands across her knees as if it would calm her down. 'I can't cope,' she said at last. 'I'm in the middle of cleaning the school. Go and get yourselves cleaned up and then go outside where you can't do any damage to the house at least!'

They turned and ran from the room as quickly as they could.

6 Problems

So far as Robert could work out, the problems were quite simple. At least, it was simple to think what they were. It was a lot harder to think of answers.

First of all, it was vital to keep the foxes secret. If anybody found out it would be the end. The village was surrounded by farms and the farmers were not great friends to foxes.

Then there was the school itself. The teachers were hardly likely to be pleased to have foxes snoring above their classrooms.

Robert said all this to Beth on the Sunday morning. He'd been thinking about it all the previous evening.

'Mrs Preston will be scared stiff of them,' Beth murmured. 'She's scared of mice. She doesn't even like spiders.'

'If she's scared of small things, just think how terrified she'll be of bigger animals,' said Robert. 'She'll probably die of fright. The bigger they are, the more scared she gets. When she sees a mouse she begins to tremble and when she sees a fox her teeth start to chatter and when she sees an elephant she screams and then a blue whale comes along and all her hair turns grey and falls out and she's shaking so much her arms and legs fall off and all that's left is a heap of bits and pieces.'

'Very funny,' Beth said stonily.

Robert frowned and added in a thoughtful tone, 'Mum would have to vacuum her up. The bits would jam up the tube.'

'Robert! Do you have to? What about the foxes?'

He smiled and then said seriously, 'We must make sure that nobody finds out about them. If there is any chance of anybody going up into the loft then we must stop them.'

'How?'

Robert turned on his sister. 'You've always got such brilliant questions, haven't you? I mean, they're really, really clever. "How?"! That's quite mind-boggling, Beth. You're the one with all the answers in class so you tell me. Come on, what's your answer, Big Brain?'

Beth listened without even blinking. As soon as Robert had finished spouting she started.

'Look, it's Sunday today –'

'Ten out of ten!' cried Robert.

'Oh shut up. It's Sunday. The foxes will probably be all right today after all that stewing steak we gave them yesterday. The parents are bound to have brought them something by now and anyway, with Mum and Dad around all day today we shan't get a chance to go up into the loft.' She paused. Robert folded his arms.

'Fine,' he said. 'That's the problem. So what's your answer?'

'We'll be back at school tomorrow. We shall have to tell our friends and they'll help us to keep an eye on the loft. We can't do it by ourselves.'

'That's all right for you,' Robert said moodily. 'You've got plenty of friends.'

Beth shrugged. 'I can't think of any other way of doing it.'

'I suppose so. I'm going out.' He fetched his bike from the side of the house and began to pedal slowly round and round the play-ground. The sun was shining, the sky was blue, and the big horse-chestnut trees were covered in growing leaves, young and green and bright. There were still some late clumps of daffodils scattered here and there around the school gardens.

Robert stopped, let his bike fall to the ground and sat down on the long bench at the end of the play area. The tiles glistened in the sun and the double chimney stood out clear and bright. Robert could see all the different specks of colour in the old red bricks. There was no sign of a fox.

It was all very well for Beth to tell her friends – she had hundreds. But who could he tell? It was easy to picture the fox, trotting across empty fields, a small piece of brown life lost in the green and blue of earth and sky. The fox had a purpose though, hunting incessantly, always returning to the same place where the fox cubs waited.

Robert glanced round the empty playground. He looked for a long time at his bike, lying on one side, cold and lifeless. What did he have? A bike. You can't talk to a bike. (Well, thought Robert, you can talk to a bike, but you'll end up in the loony-bin.) He got up and walked round to the house.

It wasn't until the evening that another problem began to niggle away in Beth's mind. After tea she took Robert to one side.

'Foxes are nocturnal,' she pointed out.

'So?'

'They come out at night and sleep during the day. That's why we've never seen the fox on the roof in daylight. That's why we've only seen it during the evening. Remember?'

Robert nodded and Beth went on. 'What it means is that they wake up at night and go running around all over the place. Suppose somebody hears them?'

Robert stared at his sister. She was right. Suppose somebody did hear them?

When they went to bed they were still worrying about it. Perhaps it was lack of sleep from the last two nights, but Robert fell into a deep dreamless sleep almost immediately. It was Beth who stayed awake and when Mum and Dad came to bed and peeped into her room she shut her eyes, pretending to be asleep.

She was still awake an hour later, but only just. Even so she jerked awake as soon as she heard the clumping and scratching. She stared out across the darkness of her room. From far away she could hear the sound of pattering and faint barking. It was unmistakeable. The foxes were playing.

The more she listened the more certain she was that Mum or Dad would wake up at any moment and realize what it was. Those foxes must be stopped!

Beth quickly got up and put on her dressing gown. She tiptoed into Robert's room and shook him by the shoulder.

'Robert! Wake up!' He rolled to one side and opened an eye.

'Mmmmmmm.'

'Wake up! The foxes are awake and making noises all over the place. What shall we do?'

Robert opened his eyes wider and lay listening to the barking and scratching above.

'I'm tired,' he mumbled.

'They're probably hungry again,' said Beth. At that moment there was a long, low howl, quickly followed by several thuds.

Robert jumped up. 'We'll give them some food to quieten them down. There are some pork chops in the fridge I think, or even some sausages.'

'We had those for tea.'

'All right. You go and get the chops and I'll put the ladder up.'

'Suppose Mum and Dad hear us?' said Beth.

'Suppose Mum and Dad hear the foxes?'

Beth squeezed her hands together and set off downstairs. Robert got his dressing gown on and fetched the aluminium stepladder. By the time he had it in place, Beth was creeping back up the stairs with two pork chops.

Robert took the meat and stuffed it into a pocket. 'You stay here,' he whispered. 'There's no point in both of us going up.'

The door scraped noisily as Robert prised

it open. He held his breath and listened for the sound of Mum and Dad waking up. Then he clambered up into the loft.

'Keep your fingers crossed,' he whispered and disappeared into the gloom of the roof.

Beth stood at the bottom of the ladder and waited. She could hear her brother crossing the rafters. She could also hear the barks and scampering leaps of the fox cubs. With the trap door wide open everything sounded deafening. Beth winced and screwed up her face as if it made it less noisy.

Mum and Dad's bed creaked. There were footsteps. Somebody was coming. There was no sign of Robert. The handle of Mum and Dad's door turned. Beth fled back into her bedroom and flung herself into bed. She tried desperately *not* to hear Dad go out on to the landing.

'Eh?' He sounded sleepy and went back into their bedroom. Beth could hear him talking to Mum.

'No, I didn't put it up. Of course I didn't. It wasn't there when we came to bed.'

Through her open doorway Beth saw Robert's unsuspecting feet appear at the top of the ladder. She wanted to cry out and warn him, but there was nothing she could do at all.

Dad shuffled back into view, doing up his dressing gown. He stopped dead and watched Robert's feet feeling their way down the cold ladder. For a second he frowned as if he couldn't work out what was happening. Then he shouted.

'Robert! What are you doing!' It was difficult to say who was the most surprised. Mum clambered out of bed and hurried to the door and watched her son slowly descend the ladder, with his back to them both.

'Robert!'

He didn't answer. He slowly came down the steps and as his feet touched the carpet he let go of the ladder and carefully turned round, holding his arms stiff out in front of him. His eyes were shut tight. He stepped forward like a robot.

Dad reached out to him, but Mum stopped him. 'Don't! He's sleepwalking. He must have been sleepwalking up there! Thank goodness he's safe. Shut up the loft quick and I'll settle him into bed.'

Robert stumbled forward towards his room. He let Mum guide him through the doorway and he tumbled into bed. Mum pulled the covers around him. She tiptoed out and went back to bed.

'He was sleepwalking,' she said to Dad.

'Up in the loft – it's daft. We'd better keep an eye on him if he's going to start walking in his sleep. I heard the noises. I thought it was burglars, or a dog. I'm sure something was barking.'

'Maybe he was barking in his sleep,' suggested Mum. 'They do all sorts of strange things in their sleep.'

They went back to bed. Beth's heart stopped thumping like a steam engine. She listened to the quiet, sleeping house. The foxes had stopped their fun and games. Mum and Dad were safe asleep. Robert was back in bed – panic over. She lay back on her pillow and closed her eyes.

7 Ham, Ham and More Ham

Robert had a hard task the next morning pretending he didn't know anything about sleepwalking in the loft. Beth kept glancing at him and he found it difficult to keep a straight face.

Dad was grouchy about the whole affair. 'You didn't even hear me when I shouted at you. What did you want to go and do a daft thing like that for?'

'I didn't know I was doing it. I was fast asleep.'

'Nobody's ever gone wandering round in their sleep before. What do you think would happen if your mum started doing it?'

What's that got to do with it? Robert

wondered. Anyhow, she'd probably look quite funny dashing about the house in her nightie and snoring her head off at the same time.

'Are you listening? I think you're fast asleep now. You're sleep-eating, Robert – hold your spoon properly, will you?' Dad glared across the table.

'I don't understand the ladder being there,' said Mum. 'He must have got the ladder out in his sleep, as well. That's really odd. Do you think we ought to take him to the doctor?'

'Huh! I don't see what a doctor can do for his table manners.'

Maybe there's a magic pill, Robert mused. Take it once a day and it turns you into a perfect human – perfect manners, perfect behaviour, perfect at school ... what a bore.

'No,' said Dad. 'You'll only have to sit for hours in the waiting room and then the doc will say, "Keep an eye on him." It's not worth the effort.'

Mum was poking about in the back of the fridge. 'I'll swear I left two pork chops in here. I bought four and we ate two last night. You children didn't have chops last night, did you? No, I remember, you finished off those sausages. Come to think of it there was some stewing steak as well.' She straightened up and put her hands on her hips. 'Hmmm. That's odd.' She stood there frowning while Beth and Robert stared at her and wondered what she was going to do. Then Mum shrugged and began to gather up the breakfast things. 'You two had better get your coats on. It's time to go round to school. And, Robert, try not to leave so much rubbish under your desk today. It took me more time to clear that than I spent on the rest of the classroom.'

Round in the playground, Beth and Robert waited for the other children to arrive. They came in little groups or singly. Mothers wandered in and out, dropping off children. Teachers arrived and began to get things ready for the week's work.

The twins gathered some friends together and went into a huddle at the far end of the playground. It was a good thing Beth was there because nobody would believe Robert.

They were so used to his fantastic stories and idiotic ideas that they assumed he was just making it all up. He wasn't exactly pleased. After all, he was the one who had heard the ghost and then worked out what it was. He was the one who'd almost killed himself on the roof and discovered the foxes' entrance to the school loft. And now it was Beth who was telling everybody.

'I want to go up there,' said Samantha.

'Me too.' There was a chorus of demands to go up and visit the fox cubs.

'Great!' cried Robert. 'Let's all go up there, the whole school. Nobody will notice. We can all go traipsing across the loft, putting our feet through the ceiling and clumping about like a herd of lost elephants. Nobody will notice!'

Mark punched Robert in the stomach and

a moment later it was all fists and feet. The others pulled them apart.

'He shouldn't be so stupid!' panted Mark, pulling his jacket straight.

'Well, honestly. How can you all go up there?' Robert shouted.

'He's right,' said Beth. 'But we will need your help. We've got to make sure that nobody else goes up there either.'

They all nodded seriously and went into school.

It was difficult to concentrate on work. Every little noise had the class sitting up, listening, and gazing at the ceiling. Mr Sykes wondered why they were all so silent. He usually spent every other breath telling somebody to be quiet. He called the register and gave it to Catherine to take to the school secretary's office.

When she came back a few minutes later she looked rather flustered. She brushed past Robert as she returned to her seat and whispered hastily in his ear.

'Go to the toilet!'

Robert wrinkled his nose and glared at her. He thought it must be some kind of insult. Catherine sat down and mouthed the same message at him. Then her lips formed into the silent word – 'Fox!'

Now he understood and got up. He crossed over to Mr Sykes.

'Can I go to the toilet please?'

'Go on. Hurry up.'

Robert went out of the room, giving a thumbs up signal to Catherine. A minute later she asked Mr Sykes if she could go to the toilet and she hurried out after Robert. He was waiting in the cloakroom.

'What's up?'

Catherine jiggled from one foot to the other as she told him.

'When I went to the secretary she was talking on the phone. She was asking for somebody to come and check the guttering on the roof. You know, that place between the two classrooms where the water runs down the wall and it spoiled our paintings.'

'Oh no!' Robert cried, as he scratched his head with both hands. 'If anybody goes up there they'll see the hole and then it will all be discovered!'

'What shall we do?' asked Catherine,

clenching her fists. 'I don't think they'll be coming today, but it was difficult to tell. I wasn't supposed to be listening.'

'No – thanks. We'll have to think of something.'

By lunchtime the entire school knew about the fox cubs – all except Mr Sykes, Mrs Preston and the infant teacher, Mrs Harvey. The story of how the cubs made too much noise at night had everybody worried. Supposing they did it again? Supposing the parent foxes couldn't find enough food to keep their children quiet?

There came a strange lunch hour. The dinner ladies were totally mystified. First of all the children pushed their meat to one side of their plate and said they didn't want it, and the next moment, when they looked again, the meat was gone. Meanwhile, the children were bent double over their tables suffering from violent stomach aches – or so it seemed.

'Whatever is the matter, Dominic?' asked one dinner lady.

'Um, nothing,' came the bright answer, as Dominic desperately tried to get a slice of cold floppy ham to stick up inside his jumper. 'I've got a bit of an itch,' he added lamely. The whole table seemed to be itching. The children were squirming and wriggling with hands up their jumpers and inside their sleeves.

'Whatever is going on?' the dinner lady demanded.

Peter tried not to sit too hard on the ham slice he'd just poked inside his trousers. 'I think somebody spilt some pepper and it's making us itchy,' he suggested. The dinner lady pressed her lips together in a thin hard line and went away.

By the end of the lunch hour sixty-eight pieces of cold ham had been hidden up jumpers, in trouser pockets, down dress fronts and Trudy even managed to put a slice inside her new white socks.

This was marvellous news for the foxes, but it became quite a problem for Robert and Beth. Children kept coming up during break and handing over scrunched-up bits of ham. Robert's pockets were stuffed full and they were beginning to feel cold and clammy against his legs.

Things did not improve back in the classroom. While they were working, different children sneaked over to Beth or Robert and slipped bits of ham on to their work books. Robert found one slice lying solemnly between the pages of his maths book.

All this ham activity made Mr Sykes suspicious. He didn't know what he was suspicious of, but there had been too many peculiar things going on. First of all the class had sat in utter silence throughout the morning. Then he'd had an extraordinary lunch-hour during which Mrs Harvey's ham vanished from her dinner plate – or so she claimed. But Mrs Harvey was so forgetful she might have eaten it without even realizing. And now children kept wandering round the classroom like lost storks looking for their nests, and they all stopped to speak to Robert or Beth. It was most odd.

Mr Sykes sat behind his desk and kept one eye on Beth. She didn't seem to be doing anything wrong, just sitting there quietly getting on with her maths. Out of the corner of his eye he saw Daphne wander past. A moment later Beth bent down under her desk.

'Beth!' She sat up quickly. The whole class stopped and waited. Mr Sykes frowned. 'What are you doing?'

'Nothing, Mr Sykes. I mean, I'm just doing my maths.'

'And what have you got in your hand?'

'Um, nothing, Mr Sykes.'

The class watched with goggle eyes. Beth never, ever got told off. She never did anything wrong – at least, not if she was being watched. Robert gazed at his sister. What if Mr Sykes went over to her desk? Suppose he came to his as well? It was stuffed full with thirty-one slices of ham. How do you explain thirty-one slices of ham? Well, you see, Mr Sykes, he could say, my mum thinks I'm too skinny and she's trying to build me up. Oh it's hopeless, thought Robert.

'Stand up, Beth. What have you got in your hand?'

Mr Sykes' voice cut across the classroom like a cutlass.

'Nothing, Mr Sykes.' Beth's face was white.

'Come here. Now show me.'

Beth stood in front of his desk. She held out her right hand and opened it, palm up. Mr Sykes nodded. 'Yes, Beth. I know there's nothing in your right hand. Now show me your left hand.'

Now she'd gone so red in the face that Robert was reminded of a bowl of tomato soup. She brought forward her tightly clenched left fist.

'Open it, Elizabeth!'

Beth slowly uncurled her fingers and there, squashed up, but plain for all to see, was a slice of cold ham.

8 What the Workman Said

Mr Sykes gazed at the pink ball of meat.
Twenty-eight pairs of eyes were glued to
Beth's back. She was beginning to sweat. So
was Robert. He fidgeted nervously in his
seat.

'Beth,' began Mr Sykes in his very soft and
dangerous kind of voice. 'Why are you
carrying a piece of ham around?'

She thought hard. Her brain felt as if it
had frozen into an icy nothingness. The only
sound that came out was a sort of hopeless
gurgle that trickled over her lips and
splattered on to the floor in a glum sludge.
She wished desperately that she was Robert
– he always had a good answer, even if it was

crazy. At least it was something to say. She had never had to stand in front of Mr Sykes' desk before and think of an excuse.

'You don't usually carry ham around with you, do you?' asked Mr Sykes. Beth shook her head. 'Well, why have you got a slice in your hand then!'

Robert suddenly waved his arm madly in the air. Mr Sykes peered past Beth and glared at her brother. 'All right, Robert. What is it?'

'It's her pet, Mr Sykes. It's for her pet.' Now everybody was staring at Robert. The whole thing was supposed to be a secret and Robert of all people was giving the game away. Paul leaned forward and poked Robert in the back.

'Shut up!' he hissed.

'What do you mean, it's for her pet?' demanded Mr Sykes.

Robert stood up. 'Beth's got a pet hedgehog that lives in the big bush by our kitchen door. She's really mad on it, Mr Sykes. She calls it Tin-Tack and she's even made a little lead for it so that she can take it for walks.' Robert was getting quite carried away. 'She gives it food every morning and every evening. Beth doesn't like ham much and she told me she was saving her ham from lunchtime to give to Tin-Tack.'

Mr Sykes gazed steadily at Robert and then he gazed steadily at Beth and then he gazed steadily at his desk. At last he spoke.

'That ham is for a hedgehog?' Beth nodded.

'Yesterday she gave it her fruit salad from teatime,' Robert called out. 'She even left the cream on.' Mr Sykes couldn't help asking if the hedgehog had eaten it. 'Only the apple bits,' said Robert.

Beth was beginning to wonder if she really did have a pet hedgehog called Tin-Tack, Robert was so convincing. Mr Sykes coughed and cleared his throat.

'I'm afraid that hedgehogs don't eat ham, Beth. At least, I don't think they do. I must say that you have been very silly and extremely naughty to take your ham from lunch. That is not what you do with school food. I think you'd better throw that horrible-looking thing in the bin. If I were you I'd ask your mother for something more suitable for a hedgehog. Now go and sit down and let's not have any more nonsense.'

Hardly believing her luck, Beth threw the slice of ham away and returned to her seat. She managed to wink at Robert as she passed. He grinned.

For a while there was peace in the classroom. It was getting near the end of the afternoon. Soon Robert and Beth would be able to clear all the ham from their desks and go and feed the foxes.

The secretary came in and a man in blue overalls followed her.

'Sorry to disturb you, Mr Sykes,' began the secretary, 'but the workman has come to look at the leaky guttering. He wanted to see where all the damage is being caused inside and Mrs Preston said it was easier to see from your classroom.'

'Of course, of course.' Mr Sykes smiled. 'It's about time something was done about it. It ruined our Egyptian display. Look, it's just up there, where there's water glistening. Do you see?'

The workman frowned and stared up at the corner of the ceiling.

'It's not so bad now,' Mr Sykes explained, 'but when it rains hard it's like a little waterfall trickling down the wall.'

'Not to worry,' said the workman. 'We'll soon have that sorted out, mate. Looks like a blocked gutter to me. I'll just get the ladder and pop up there to clear it.'

A faint murmur ran through the class. The children looked at each other wildly. They must do something. The workman had already gone outside to fetch his ladder.

Jason waved his hand around. 'Please, Mr Sykes, is it safe up there on the roof?'

'What do you mean?'

Jason turned pink. 'I just wondered if it was safe ... if he was going up there ... if he'd be safe ...' His effort fell to pieces as Mr Sykes began to laugh.

'Of course it's safe up there,' he said.

'But, Mr Sykes,' interrupted Christine, 'it might not be as safe as it was before. I mean, it might not be as safe now as it was safe when it was safe before, if you see what I mean.'

'I do not see what you mean, Christine, and you are talking pure rubbish.'

'The roof might be safe,' murmured

Greg, 'but the ladder might not be.'

By this time the workman had returned to have another glance at the damage inside. He stopped and looked at Greg with some concern.

'The ladder might have some rungs missing,' said Greg. Michelle spoke up.

'My dad's ladder has got some rungs missing.'

'Just what are you all going on about?' cried Mr Sykes. 'Why are you all so worried about the workman? I am sure the roof is quite safe and his ladder is in perfect condition, isn't it?'

The workman jerked himself straight and nodded vigorously.

'Oh, er, yes, I think so. I'm sure it is!' he said

'That's what my uncle said,' muttered Adam darkly.

Mr Sykes eyed him for a moment. 'What do you mean?' he asked at last.

'My uncle said his ladder was all right, but when he went up it the rungs broke. They had woodworm. He fell down and broke his leg and his arm.'

'Adam!'

'He did, Mr Sykes, and he was in hospital for months and months because the bones didn't heal properly, or something like that, and the doctors had to break his arm and leg all over again and he couldn't –'

'Adam!' By this time both Mr Sykes and the workman had turned a whitish green. 'I don't want to hear any more nonsense.' Mr Sykes gave the workman a sickly smile. 'I think you'd better get on with it before the children come up with any more wild ideas.'

The workman seemed pleased to get out of the classroom with all his bones in one piece. A minute or so later the children could see him through the classroom window, climbing up his aluminium ladder and out of sight.

Mr Sykes began to read them a story. The minutes ticked by and there was still no sign of the workman. Everybody was looking out of the window. There was a faint sound of scraping from above.

At last the ladder rattled and they saw the workman's feet and then his body and head as he came down, carrying a plastic bucket in one hand.

The secretary came out from her office and spoke to him. They both came round to the classroom. The workman scratched his head and peered into the bucket.

'Did you find the cause?' asked Mr Sykes.

'Gutter was blocked, all right,' began the workman. 'There were all these droppings up there, and a pile of feathers too.'

Mr Sykes looked into the bucket. 'Bird droppings I suppose?' The workman shook his head.

'No, no. Much too big for bird droppings. I thought maybe it was a dog, but a dog couldn't get up there. Not right on to that roof.'

'Perhaps it was a cat?' suggested the secretary.

'Too big for a cat.' The workman shook his head. 'Nope. There's only one creature I know as would do something like that.'

'Yes?'

'A fox.'

'A fox!'

'Yeah. It's an easy climb for a fox. Anyway, I've cleared up there for the time being. I shall have to come back tomorrow.

Secretary here ought to ring through to the pest control people at the council. They'll come down tomorrow morning and we'll see what's what up there.'

'Well I never!' murmured Mr Sykes. 'A fox on the roof!' He was cut short by the bell for the end of school.

The children put their chairs up so that the classroom could be cleaned easily and then they began making their way home. Everybody spoke to Beth and Robert.

'What are you going to do?' It was the same question, over and over again. Beth just looked gloomy and couldn't think of anything to say at all. She carefully removed all the ham slices stored in her desk and transferred them to her bag.

'What are you going to do, Robert?'

He turned on the cluster of boys around him. 'What do you think I'm going to do? I'm going to get my machine gun and stand guard over them and shoot anybody who comes near them? What do you think I'm going to do?'

The truth was that he had no idea at all. He felt helpless. He didn't know anybody who could do anything now. He grabbed his bag full of ham and went round to the house. Mum was already preparing to clean the school. Dad was out at work.

Robert didn't wait for Beth. He got the little ladder out and went straight up to the house loft, scrambling down into the school loft and hurrying forward to the chimney. There he stopped.

Four pairs of eyes glowed at him through the darkness, blinking occasionally. It must be the mother, Robert thought, watching from a distance. The mother seemed enormous. She was a deep, ruddy red and had streaks of mud down one flank.

She raised her head and eyed Robert. She didn't seem afraid and the cubs didn't whimper in the way they usually did when he approached. Robert got out the ham and moved several steps closer. The mother pricked up her ears and never took her eyes off him. She bunched her front legs further beneath her.

'I'm not going to hurt you,' Robert whispered. 'Look, I've brought you some ham.' He held the meat in front of him, swung his arm back and tossed the ham forward. It landed with a plop in front of the mother. Very slowly she lowered her muzzle and sniffed at it, still watching Robert intently. Then she sank back on her haunches and began to lick the meat.

The cubs started to make strange noises and edged forward to their mother. They looked so defenceless. Robert was overcome with a desire to gather them up and protect them somehow. He began to edge carefully forward. The mother lifted her head and watched him warily.

9 The Earth in the Sky

'I won't hurt you,' Robert murmured. The vixen lifted one paw and covered the ham slices as if she thought Robert would take them away from her. Her lips curled back a little and she gave a quiet snarl. The three cubs were making little jumps at the ham, pouncing on it and tearing it with their claws. Then they would have a quick chew.

Robert crossed to the next rafter and hovered, trying to keep his balance and watching the big vixen all the time, while she watched him. Now he was just a metre or two from the family. He wondered where the dog-fox was and if he would reappear suddenly. He stepped forward and slowly crouched down, steadying himself against the slope of the roof.

The vixen chewed on the ham. She had her back to the old cupboard. One of the cubs had gone inside, leaving the other two to continue their feast. Robert reached out his hand, steadily and slowly. The sharp tang of the fox family filled his nostrils, all mixed up with the must and dust of the loft. He could see the sharp teeth snapping at the meat and the long pink tongues like squashed fingers, curling round the scraps.

'I won't hurt you,' he repeated, his hand moving closer and closer. Then his fingers touched the fluff of the big cub. Just two fingers touching!

Robert grinned madly in the darkness and the vixen's yellow eyes never left his face. He scratched the cub lightly across the shoulders and on the top of his head. The cub flattened himself against the ground and squinted. Then he opened his mouth wider and wider and gave a long, moaning yawn, finally shutting his jaws with a little snap.

Robert gently began to stroke the cub's back, using his fingers to scratch his back at the same time. Gradually Robert edged nearer still. He slipped his other hand gently beneath the cub's belly and began to lift him up. The cub turned and looked at Robert with startled, wide eyes, and his four paws dangled in mid-air giving little kicks.

The mother sat up, alert and ready to leap to the cub's defence. But Robert settled the cub on his lap and went on softly stroking the little creature. Again the cub closed his eyes and laid his muzzle across Robert's leg. It was the most incredible feeling that Robert had ever had – simple and overwhelming. Like God at the creation of the earth, he thought.

He grinned. Wasn't a fox's home called an earth? And here he was, watching the earth, the earth in the sky and the fox on the roof!

His thoughts were disturbed by a noise from the far end of the loft. He stared out into the darkness, wondering if Mum had come up to find him. He heard stumbling steps getting closer.

'Robert! Robert!' It was Beth. 'Are you up here?'

He didn't want to speak in case he

disturbed the foxes. She reached the big chimney and looked round.

'Oh!' She stood and looked unbelievingly at Robert sitting by the old cupboard with the cub asleep on his lap and the vixen alert but quiet next to him.

'Don't come any closer,' Robert whispered. 'You might frighten her and she'll probably bite me. I'd better leave him anyhow.'

He gently lifted the cub and put him beside the vixen. Then he ever so slowly got to his feet and went across to Beth. He took the rest of the ham from her and put it by the cupboard.

'We'd better leave them now,' he said, and his voice was full of a satisfaction he'd not experienced before.

As they climbed down the ladder and on to the landing he kept saying over and over again, inside his head, 'I've held a live fox cub! I've picked up a real, wild fox and stroked it and held it and sat next to the mother. I have! I've really done it, myself!'

Throughout the evening he was quiet, so much so that when Dad came in he thought Robert was sickening for something.

'I'm all right.' Robert laughed, feeling again the warmth of the cub inside him, like an invisible hug. When he went to bed he fell into a deep and undisturbed sleep. It was Beth who tossed all night worrying about the foxes and what would happen when the workman returned.

The next morning the whole school was on edge waiting for the workman and the pest control people to arrive. Nobody knew when to expect them. The teachers could tell something was up because the atmosphere in the classrooms was charged and tense. But they had no idea *what* was up.

At half past eleven the trouble started. There was a loud, unearthly howl. It floated slowly down from the ceiling like an invisible blanket. Mr Sykes put down his pen.

'I don't think we need any noises like that, thank you,' he said curtly, and picked up his pen once more. The children looked at each other and held their breath.

Another low howl lifted through the air and drifted across the emptiness by the ceiling. Robert's heart had tumbled down into his socks and was burrowing its way frantically into his toes. A terrible coldness brought his skin up in goosepimples.

'Is that you, Robert? You look as if you've seen a ghost.'

Suddenly Greg threw himself across the top of his desk and groaned loudly. 'Aaaaaaagh!' It didn't sound much like the fox in the loft, but it convinced Mr Sykes for a moment.

'Aaaaaagh!' Greg scowled furiously and clutched his stomach.

'Whatever is the matter, Greg?' Mr Sykes jumped up.

'It's my ooooooh! My stomach! I think I've got appendicitis. Yurrrrgh!'

Mr Sykes frowned and bent over the fallen Greg. Even as he did so there was the sound of tremendous bumping and scraping from above. A yowling chorus of growls made the ceiling rattle and it was quickly followed by a mad pounding of feet going round and round above everybody's head.

Mr Sykes forgot all about Greg's effort to attract his attention. 'Don't worry, class, I'll sort this out!' He made for the door. Robert and Beth sprang from their seats and planted themselves in front of it. 'Out of the way, you two,' Mr Sykes cried.

Another wild chase started up in the loft. The fox cubs were obviously having a great game up there. A little trickle of dust floated down.

'Will you two get out of the way?'

'Sorry, Mr Sykes,' said Beth, falling to one knee. 'I was just tying my shoelaces.' He didn't seem to notice that Beth had buckles on her shoes.

'Mr Sykes, Mr Sykes,' Robert began. 'Are you sure you ought to go out there? I'm sure it's not safe for you ...'

'Whatever are you talking about?'

'I'm sure it's dangerous for you. It was in your horoscope this morning.' Robert kept talking desperately. 'I remember reading it in the paper.'

'What utter rubbish. You're talking gibberish. You don't even know what sign I am.'

'I do! You're a Taurus, the bull.' It was a wild guess.

'How do you know that? For goodness sake, why am I having this daft conversation with you? Just get out of the way!' Mr Sykes forced his way to the door and went out. A moment later he returned with a long ladder.

By this time Mrs Preston, the headmistress, had come into the room.

'Just stop all that noise, children. Mr Sykes, there seem to be strange noises from up above. Oh, you've got the ladder.'

'I'm just going up there,' said Mr Sykes grimly. He positioned the ladder against the trap door in the classroom ceiling and climbed up. The ghostly howls were even louder when the door was flung back. A cloud of dust fell down on the children below and they started coughing and spluttering. Mr Sykes had his head and shoulders in the loft and his feet on the ladder.

'I thought it must be pigeons,' he called out. 'But they're the strangest pigeons I've ever heard. I'm going right up.'

So saying he hauled his legs up through the trap door and disappeared from sight. Now there wasn't a sound from above except Mr Sykes' shuffling steps as he made his way across the loft. Robert buried his face in his arms. He couldn't bear to watch or listen.

All at once there was chaos. Pounding feet and snarling and growling. A distant voice yelled out.

'There's a bloomin' fox up here! No! Two, three, five foxes! Argh! Get off, will you, get off!'

There was a loud crash and a pile of plaster showered down from the ceiling. A long hairy leg appeared through the ceiling with a brown shoe kicking furiously at one end. It wriggled and writhed while children screamed and more and more plaster hurtled down from the gap and splattered across desks and floor.

At last Mr Sykes managed to free his leg and he came racing down the ladder as if he were being chased by the entire cast of a horror film. He stood shaking and trembling, with blood trickling down his leg and the side of his face.

'There's a family of foxes up there!' he blurted.

Mrs Preston stared at him aghast. 'So the workman *was* right! Oh dear, Mr Sykes, we can't have foxes up in the school loft. They're vermin! They carry all sorts of diseases.

There'll be rats and all sorts of things next!'

Mr Sykes wiped his scratched face with a paper tissue. 'The pest control people will sort them out,' he said.

'Yes, I suppose so. They'll gas them I should think. There's no hope of moving the creatures. They'll have to be gassed.'

Robert was out of his seat like a fighter pilot. 'You can't!' he yelled. 'You can't just go round doing things like that. They're not doing any harm up there. You can't!'

'That's enough, Robert,' snapped Mrs Preston. 'They're vermin.'

'But they weren't doing any harm until you went up there. And that workman too. If they hadn't been disturbed you would never have known. Why don't you leave them alone?'

Mr Sykes regarded Robert curiously. 'How long have you known about these foxes, Robert?' he asked.

Robert looked at the plaster on the floor. 'Since Thursday,' he mumbled at last. Mr Sykes sighed and nodded.

'Ah! First there were ghosts and then there was sleepwalking and then that strange lunchtime and the business with the ham – it all makes sense now.' Mrs Preston pressed her lips together.

'Hmmph. Well, it doesn't make sense to me, Mr Sykes. Perhaps you'd ...'

'Look!' screamed Wendy. 'Look – the foxes!' Wendy was staring out of the window. Everybody rushed over. There, out on the playground were the foxes, all five of them. The parents were trotting along purposefully, each with a cub in its mouth. The biggest cub was bouncing up and down alongside, frantically trying to keep up.

Robert felt as if somebody had just sliced through all the ropes that bound him tight. 'They're going,' he whispered. 'They're going, Beth.'

'They're going all right,' said Mr Sykes. 'Going to find a new home. I imagine they found life in the school loft a little too hectic – and I can't say I'm surprised.' He began to laugh. Mrs Preston and the children gazed at him with wonder. His trouser leg was torn and there was still blood on his face and leg and he was laughing louder and louder. The more Mr Sykes realized what had been going on, the louder he laughed.

The fox family reached the far end of the playground and slipped through the fencing and into the field beyond. Their tails disappeared. They were gone.

Robert smiled. They were safe and they'd gone. But what hadn't gone was something that would never go and nobody could ever change. Last night he had sat with the vixen and held the big cub. He gazed out of the big window at the empty playground and the fields beyond.

Behind him the children had all started laughing. Mr Sykes had sat down because he couldn't stand up and laugh any longer. Mrs Preston just seemed astonished by the whole affair.

'Perhaps when you've recovered,' she said to the red-faced Mr Sykes, 'you could tell me what the joke is, Mr Sykes.'

'Joke,' he spluttered. 'There isn't a joke. At least, not one joke. There are hundreds of them!' And he and the class began giggling all over again.

Robert grinned too. It was one story he hadn't made up.